Looking Up

Looking Up

ABENA EYESON

Cover designed by Dissect Design

www.dissectdesigns.com

This book is a work of fiction. Names, characters, places, and incidents either are products of the author's imagination or are used fictitiously. Any resemblance to actual persons, living or dead, events, or locales is entirely coincidental.

Published by AE Press

www.abenaeyesonwrites.com

The right of Abena Eyeson to be identified as the author of this work has been asserted by her in accordance with the Copyright, Designs and Patents Act 1988

Printed in the United States of America

First Printing: January 2019

Typeset in Merriweather

Printed and bound by KDP

First Edition

ISBN- 978-1-9160004-0-7

ACKNOWLEDGEMENTS

Thank you to Ato, Ekua, Araba and Kojo for their support and patience whilst I wrote this book. Thank you also to Kofi and Eugenia for their support whilst editing the book.

1

Why has Nana Nancy not turned the ceiling fan on? Doesn't she feel the heat? There is a slight breeze from the open louvre blades in the windows facing the veranda, but still, the living room is so hot, almost as hot as it is outside.

Nana hasn't even noticed that I've walked in. Sitting on her favourite sofa, the brown leather one made by Mr Osei, the furniture maker, down the road, she's staring into space, deep in thought, as she hums to herself.

Nana loves this living room, full of furniture, family photos and ornaments. In fact, she loves this house which she inherited from her parents when they died many years ago and in which she raised Mummy and Auntie Cissy. I've heard Nana talk many times about how much the house means to her. I have to say that the house means a lot to me too. Since the age of four, it's been a place where I've felt loved, safe and happy. Every time I walk in, I have this warm sensation and feel like I'm home.

Smiling, I say, "Good afternoon Nana Nancy," as I walk towards her.

Her face lights up as she turns to me, looking much younger than her sixty-three years of age. "Oh, good Esi, you're home. Come and sit down, my dear," she says, patting the seat next to her. "I have good news."

Wondering what the news could be, I go and sit beside her.

"Esi, Maggie called this morning," Nana says, looking excited as she clasps both my hands in hers.

Baffled as to why this is big news as Mummy often calls, I ask, "How is Mummy?"

"She is well, Esi, and sends her love, but the reason why she called is that she has finally sorted things out so you can go and live with her in London. She is sending the money for your plane ticket and at the end of August, you will be flying out to join her!" Nana's eyes sparkle with happiness.

I smile at her, as she is clearly expecting me to be pleased with the news. But, in truth, I don't feel exactly happy, more ... shocked. I wasn't expecting this at all. Mummy has been working in London so long that I've gotten used to her living there and me living here with Nana.

"But that means that in less than three months' time, I'll be leaving." The words slip out of my mouth as it dawns on me.

"Yes, Esi," says Nana with a big smile. "In less than three months time, you will be living with your Mummy once again. Thanks be to God."

But I'm not thanking God. Panic is making my head pound as I think about leaving Nana, Ama, Auntie Cissy, this house and everything I know behind to go to London by myself.

I don't want that!

Yes, it would be nice to see Mummy but I don't want to live in London. I'm happy living right here!

Nana carries on talking, oblivious to my turmoil. "How I've been praying for Maggie to send for you. Every child should live with their mother, Esi. It has worried me that you and Maggie have lived apart for years."

Letting go of my hands, she picks up the white handkerchief on her lap and mops her forehead before waving it in the air, saying, "Thank you God for answering my prayers."

She leans on the armrest and pushes herself up to her feet. "*Da n'ase, Da n'ase, Da Onyame ase,*" she starts to sing, thanking God. Swaying from side to side, she slowly makes her way around the large wooden centre table, singing and waving her handkerchief in the air, her brown sandals tapping the terrazzo floor.

"Eh Mama, you're in fine voice this afternoon," Auntie Cissy says beaming at Nana. Auntie Cissy looks just like a younger version of Nana – slender and petite with a kind face. She and Ama have just walked into the living room. When we arrived from school a short while ago, I headed straight to the living room, but Auntie Cissy went to speak to Irene in the kitchen while Ama disappeared upstairs to use the bathroom.

Nana stops singing to happily tell them the news, adjusting her green head tie as she does so. Auntie Cissy and Ama start to jubilate loudly before rushing over to hug me. Ama links her arm through mine and sits down beside me. Auntie Cissy shakes her curly weave from side to side and sings loudly, as she follows Nana who has started singing and dancing around the centre table again.

"You're so lucky, Cuz," Ama says, resting her cornrowed head on my shoulder.

"I don't feel lucky," I say grumpily, absolutely certain I'd much rather stay here than go to London.

"C'mon Esi. Of course, you are. I wish I could go to London." Ama smiles and winks, her dimpled face looking at me. "Maybe you can put me in your suitcase when you go. I'm sure nobody will notice. I'm only small after all."

3

I smile at her as she laughs, wishing I *could* take her with me. I would be much happier about moving to London if she was coming.

Ama starts to clap for Nana and Auntie Cissy as they dance and sing. Then she gets up to join them, singing at the top of her voice and shaking herself vigorously in her blue and white school dress, which is oversized like mine.

The intense afternoon heat has them sweating before too long. Damp patches appear in Nana's green *kaba* and Auntie Cissy's white work blouse. But they don't stop.

I don't move. I can't move.

I'm biting my tongue to stop myself screaming at them, "I don't want to go. I don't want to leave you!"

But I can't say it out loud. Look at them. They won't understand.

So, with a smile fixed on my face, I watch them as a feeling of dread settles in the pit of my tummy.

2

The time and date on my watch glow in the dark. I should be asleep, but I'm wide awake.

For most of the flight, I've been transfixed by the small TV screen in front of me. It's my first time on an airplane and the novelty of being able to watch as many films as I want on my personal screen has been hard to resist. I swear, Ama will be green with envy when I tell her about the movies I've seen. My last movie, *102 Dalmatians*, has just come to an end.

I rub my tired eyes and take my headphones off. Leaning back in my window seat, I wriggle about to get more comfortable. It's cool in the cabin, very different from the warm evening air in Accra before we boarded the plane. No, warm is not the right word. Balmy. That's it. I learnt that word only the other day and the evening air in Accra was definitely balmy.

I fold my arms to warm them up. I wish I'd listened to Nana Nancy about wearing my yellow knitted cardigan and black trousers. The blue tie-dye top and trousers that I insisted on wearing are not keeping me very warm. The black jacket Nana gave me would help, but I left it in my rucksack which is in the overhead luggage compartment, so I can't get to it. Remembering that I'm sitting on my British Airways blanket, I lift myself up and grab it. Sitting down again, I open out the blanket and wrap it tightly around me. Hopefully, this will warm me up soon.

I look around the economy class cabin, noticing how quiet and dark it's become. The only lights I see are that of the odd TV screen and overhead lamp. I must be one of the few people still awake on this flight to London from Accra.

Suddenly, it hits me. I'm on my own. I've left Nana, Ama and Auntie Cissy. For as long as I can remember, they have been the ones who have been there for me. How am I going to manage without them? My throat tightens as tears of panic fill my eyes.

Battling my feelings, I stare out of my window. The lights of Accra have long disappeared, and darkness is all I see from the window, apart from the plane's flashing lights. I want to sob but I'm surrounded by all these strangers. It would be embarrassing if they were woken up by me crying like a baby.

A loud snort makes me jump. I look at the old black American lady, asleep and snoring, in the aisle seat next to me. Before she fell asleep, her chatter was comforting at first. I'd been feeling nervous about being on the flight by myself until she sat next to me. But after a while, her talking got a little irritating as she just wouldn't stop, even when I was trying to watch TV. I was definitely relieved when she fell asleep.

Watching TV has been a good distraction. For a while at least, it has stopped me thinking about my move to London. It's not that I've anything against London or living with Mummy for that matter. I would just rather still be living with Nana Nancy, Ama and Auntie Cissy in Tesano and not be having to give up everything I know to go and live somewhere I know nothing about.

Plus, I haven't lived with Mummy since I was six and I'm now thirteen! Yes, she calls from time to time to speak to me and in fact, this last week she's called virtually every day to make sure everything was in place for my trip and that I knew what to do when I got to the airport. But that's not the same as living with her. The last time I actually saw her was three years ago when she came to Ghana for two weeks for Nana Nancy's sixtieth birthday. During that visit, relatives descended on the house most days wanting to see her as they hadn't seen her for a long time. Between that, Nana's big party at the Tesano Methodist Church Hall, Mummy seeing her friends and the shopping she insisted on doing, I didn't even get to spend that much time with her.

Nana Nancy has told me many times that I'm lucky and that Mummy has worked hard to give me the opportunity to go to London. Even at the airport, she said, "Esi, *wo kɔ tena aburokyire.*"

"I know I'm going to live abroad, Nana," I said through clenched teeth.

"Not everyone gets that chance, Esi. Many children in Ghana would give their right hand to be in your shoes. You are so fortunate."

It's not that I don't want to feel excited about going to live in London. I do, but all I feel is ... anxious. Yes, that's it. Anxious.

My eyes fill with tears again.

I've cried so much already. At the airport, Ama and I clung to each other in tears. Since we were both four, we've done everything together including sharing a room and going to the same school. Now, we didn't even know when we were going to see each other again.

Is this how I felt when Mummy first left for London?

I don't actually remember. Somehow, my brain has blocked it out. But Nana told me that I clung to Mummy and sobbed all the way to the airport that day, reducing Mummy to tears. Nothing said calmed me down. At the airport, she had to prise me off Mummy, telling her firmly to go. According to Nana, when we got home, Ama had been allowed by Auntie Cissy to stay up and wait for me.

When I was carried into the living room, she was there with her arms out. Stepping away from Nana, I walked into Ama's arms and, apparently, she said, "Esi, we have each other. Mummy and Nana are here, too. We will look after you. It will be okay."

And it was okay. So much so that after I heard in June that I was moving to London, I prayed every day that something would happen that would mean that I didn't have to go. I prayed that Mummy would return to live in Ghana instead and life would carry on as normal. But my prayers were all in vain, as here I am on my way to London.

"Hello, dear."

Startled, I look up to see a smiling blonde air hostess reaching for the empty cup on my fold down table. "Would you like another drink?"

Forcing a smile, I say, "Apple juice, please."

She hands me my apple juice and says, "Try and get some sleep, dear."

I nod and smile again, with no intention of complying. With all that is going on in my head, how can I sleep? I drink my apple juice quickly, savouring the sweet taste and momentarily forgetting my worries. In Ghana, I rarely got to drink apple juice. It's expensive because it's imported so Nana and Auntie Cissy would only buy it occasionally as a treat. So I'm enjoying drinking as much of it as possible on the plane.

Putting my cup down, I catch sight of the family sleeping in the middle row along from me. I've been watching the father and his two children on and off since the plane took off. The father's attentiveness to his children has been fascinating. I wish I had a father like that. I don't even know my father, nor his side of the family. The only things I know about my father are that I have his

8

surname, my middle name Asantewa is his mother's name, and Mummy left him when I was four years old.

Mummy never talks about him. Nana and Auntie Cissy say that Mummy is the one who should tell me about him and that she will, eventually. But when is that going to be?

As I've not seen my father since Mummy left him, I can't even recollect what he looks like. Every time I see other children with their fathers, I remember that I've got a father but he plays no part in my life and I don't know why. I often wonder what he looks like, what he is doing and why he has never come to see me? Doesn't he care about me at all?

Thinking about my father makes my chest feel tight. This often happens when I think about him. I close my eyes and rub my chest, trying to get rid of the tightness and the bitter feeling of rejection.

Maybe ... when I'm living with Mummy, she might decide to tell me about him.

That sudden glimmer of something to look forward to begins to ease the pain. I stop rubbing but my eyelids feel heavy and stay closed. Imagining what it would be like to know more about my father, I slowly drift off to sleep.

3

Stepping off the plane with my jacket on and my blue rucksack on my back, I file into the airport with the many other passengers getting off the flight. Unlike me, most of them walk off briskly as if they know where they are going. The black American lady walks so fast that soon I lose track of her.

Feeling a little daunted by the sheer size of what I see, I trudge behind the other passengers. Yesterday, Kotoka airport looked large but Heathrow seems enormous. There are so many bright lights and everything looks new and modern. I walk for what feels like an age, my black, sling-backs getting more and more uncomfortable. I like these shoes, but if I'd known I'd be walking so much, I would have worn my white trainers instead, then my feet wouldn't be hurting as much as they are now.

Suddenly, I spot people ahead of me stepping onto something that looks like a large conveyor belt on the floor. It moves them along as they stand on it. Brilliant! I hurry to the conveyor belt and stand on it too, glad to be able to stop walking for a while. The contraption doesn't move very fast, but still, it comes to an end far too soon and I have to get off and start walking again.

Finally, I reach the area signposted "Immigration." I join the long winding queue next to the sign "Non-EU passengers," as Nana and Mummy had told me to. It takes about half an hour for me to get to the front of the queue where I'm called forward by a large white man sitting behind a desk who asks for my passport. He starts to look through it, page by page. I wonder what he is looking at when the passport is brand new. This is my first ever trip out of Ghana, so apart from my British visa which Nana went with me to get from the British High Commission in Accra, there is nothing much to see in the passport.

"What is your name?" he asks sternly.

"Esi Asantewa Addo, sir," I reply.

"Are you travelling by yourself?

"Yes, sir."

"How old are you?"

"Thirteen, sir."

"What brings you to London?"

"I have come to join my mother, sir. She lives here."

"Hmm," he says.

What does that mean?

"Did anyone give you anything to bring?" he asks.

"No, sir," I say, though I then wonder whether I should mention the *kenkey* and *shito* Nana Nancy packed in my suitcase after cooking it especially for Mummy. But, looking at his face, I decide it's best not to say anything.

The man looks at my passport some more before stamping it and handing it back to me. I take my passport but can't remember what to do next.

The man looks at me questioningly before saying with a slight smile, "Follow the signs to the luggage hall."

Grateful for the help, I flash him a smile before following the signs.

Stepping off the moving stairs (which are so cool), I arrive at the luggage hall and spot the black man and his two children who were sitting along from me on the plane. They are standing by a large, circular looking thing on which luggage is going round and round. That must be where I go for my suitcases. I head there, stopping to get a trolley on the way after seeing other people doing the same.

After a short wait, I see one of my suitcases. I grab it and struggle to get it onto the trolley. I look up to see my second suitcase about to whiz past, so I run for it but, luckily, the man with the kids gets it for me.

"Let me put it on the trolley for you," he says with a kind smile.

"Thank you," I say, relieved.

He deposits the case on the trolley and says, "Take care," before walking back to his children. I can't help but wonder if my father would be like that.

I notice people pushing their trolleys through a green exit marked "Nothing to declare" and remember that Mummy had told me to use that exit. Pushing my trolley through the green exit, I end up in an area where many people are waiting behind barriers.

I move my trolley forward for a bit before stopping to look for Mummy in the crowd of people. Then, out of the crowd walks a plump, black woman with long plaits wearing jeans, a white T-shirt and a black cardigan. When she calls out, "Esi" and waves at me, I realise it's Mummy. As I near her, I see that in some ways, she's still the mother I remember, but in other ways, she has changed. The mother I knew was always made up, immaculately dressed with high heels and a fancy hairdo. But the Mummy I see now has no makeup on, her long plaits are simply worn and she is wearing blue trainers. Wow, I've never seen Mummy in trainers before.

When she reaches me, she pulls me into a tight embrace with a large smile, saying, "*Akwaaba*, Esi. It's so good to see you."

Mummy's joy at seeing me gives me a warm feeling and some of my anxiety eases.

Loosening her grip, she gazes at my face. "Look at how much you've grown. You are such a big girl now. How was the flight?"

"Okay," I say, suddenly feeling tongue-tied and not sure of what to say next.

"Good. I was worried about you travelling by yourself, but Mama insisted that you would be fine. I guess she was right. C'mon, let's go. We are going to catch the bus back to my flat."

Mummy starts pushing my trolley and I follow her. But the walk, past airport shops and lots of people, is long. I'm tired and my feet hurt even more. Finally, we emerge at a bustling bus station. After buying bus tickets from a machine, Mummy looks out at the buses before saying, "Hurry Esi. Our bus is already here." She lifts my suitcases off the trolley and drags them behind her as she rushes for the bus. I keep up with her. When we reach the bus, there is already a queue of people getting on it.

Despite my tiredness, I'm excited. We're getting on a red double-decker bus like the buses I've seen in movies set in the UK. I can't wait to tell Ama about this. Buses are a novelty. Apart from coaches on school trips, I've never been in one. Most of the time in Ghana, I was driven everywhere in Auntie Cissy's car by her driver.

As Mummy steps onto the bus ahead of me, I watch in amazement as she lugs both my suitcases onto the bus. Is this how things are done in London? In Ghana, Mummy wouldn't have been carrying cases. There would have been somebody who would have carried them on for her for a small tip. Still stunned, I walk onto the bus as Mummy flashes our tickets at the bus driver. He closes the bus doors behind me.

Mummy proceeds to pull my cases past standing passengers into a recessed area not far from the bus driver. The bus sets off with a lurch, forcing me to grab hold of a metal pole. Mummy says, "Sit down," and points to the two vacant seats next to the recessed area. I do as I'm told, sitting by the window with my rucksack still strapped to my back. "Alright?" she asks as she sits next to me. I nod and smile.

"You must be really tired," she says. "We should be at my flat in about half an hour and then you can rest."

"Okay," I reply, not knowing what else to add. I don't know why I feel at such a loss as to what to say to Mummy. Maybe it's because it feels weird being here with her. I haven't been with her on my own for such a long time. I turn to look out of the window, resting my head on the glass.

The bus makes its way slowly down a road busy with other vehicles trying to leave Heathrow airport. I spot cars, vans, buses and black taxis like the ones I've seen in films. It definitely feels strange being in London seeing things I've only ever seen on screen before.

After making its way through a tunnel, the bus finally ends up going down a road that looks like a motorway, but this motorway is so orderly. The only motorway I've seen in Ghana is the one between Accra and Tema. People on that motorway don't drive like this. There, they drive as they please, beeping their horn and overtaking. Here, I've not even heard one horn being beeped yet. I can see drivers using their car indicators and waiting for space before moving lanes.

14

Wow! From the little I've seen of London so far, it's so different from Accra.

The bus comes off the motorway and starts stopping at bus stops along the road. Soon I see a large sign with *Welcome to Uxbridge* printed on it. The bus drives past houses and high-rise buildings that look like flats. The orderliness on the road seems to extend to buildings too, as a lot of them look similar. In Accra, you could drive down a road and most of the houses you see will have their own individual look.

I sneak a quick look at Mummy. I'm conscious that I'm not saying anything to her but then neither is she saying anything to me. Her round face and big eyes still look attractive, but I can see worry lines on her forehead. She doesn't look much like Nana or Auntie Cissy. Not only is Mummy bigger but her skin is a bit lighter too. I think she took after her father, Nana's husband, who died when Mummy and Auntie Cissy were children. I've seen photos of him in Nana's living room and there is definitely a resemblance. Mummy glances at me and smiles.

"You alright?" she asks once more.

I nod my head but turn to look out of the window again. Though I'm happy with the warmth she is showing me, I'm still struggling to know what to say to her.

The bus drives past a *Welcome to Hayes and Harlington* sign. The roads are quiet, definitely not as busy as the traffic jammed roads in Accra would be by now. We go past many shops and, down a paved shopping area, I glimpse a canopied enclosure that looks like the bandstands I've seen in films. I spot many restaurants with names that suggest they serve food from countries other than the UK.

London, so far, is surprising.

15

From what I can see inside and outside the bus, it seems people from all over the world are here. There are many skin colours, styles of clothing and, in the bus, different languages being spoken. This is not how I pictured London. I thought most people would be white and speak English like the Queen but as yet, I've not heard anyone speaking English like the Queen.

The bus turns left off a main road onto a long residential road.

"We are getting off here," says Mummy, as she gets up and presses a red button on the metal pole in front of her. She pulls my suitcases towards the exit door and I follow her. Soon we are standing on the pavement as the bus pulls away.

Gusts of cool morning air have me zipping up my coat. I'm so glad Nana gave me this to wear. How come it's so cold, anyway? Isn't it supposed to be summer? The sun is shining but it's not providing much heat.

"Come Esi, my flat is just here." Mummy pulls my suitcases across the quiet road towards a row of houses on the other side. I follow and stand next to her as she stops at a house joined on both sides by other houses. The house oddly has two doors – one turquoise with a silver 5 on it and the other black with a silver 5A on it. Mummy glances at me and smiles. "Esi, welcome to your new home."

4

"I thought you lived in a flat?" I ask, confused.

Mummy laughs. "I do. This is a house divided into two flats. I live in the top flat and my landlady, Comfort, lives at the bottom with her family."

"Oh, I see," I say, although I don't really.

How different this is from Nana's house. Though I'm miles away, I can clearly picture the white, colonial, two storey house in Tesano with its high compound walls topped by coiled razor-sharp wire to keep burglars out. The gravel drive at the front leads from the compound gates to a wide veranda. The back garden that Ama and I loved to play in is full of fruit trees and flowers, including every shade of bougainvillaea imaginable as they are Nana's favourite flower.

The small glass-fronted building that houses Nana's bakery is next to the compound gates. People from all over Accra come to order cakes from the bakery for weddings, birthdays and christenings. The bakery was a favourite hangout for Ama and I. How I loved the smell of baking bread and cakes. Even now, as I close my eyes, I can instantly remember the smell.

"What are you doing, Esi? Come on. Let's go in." Mummy's voice makes me jump.

I open my eyes, feeling a little disorientated, to find her standing by the open black front door. I hurry after her and walk in. As Mummy pulls the cases in and closes the door, I look around the small hall. The hall is the only space on the ground floor. From it, stairs lead up to the first floor.

Bare and dull.

That is what strikes me as I look around. The plain beige walls are unadorned and the carpet is a dark indistinguishable colour. As I walk up the stairs, the first door I come to leads into a compact kitchen with a smallish window. The kitchen has yellow walls, white kitchen cabinets, and a dark tiled floor.

Next door to the kitchen is a modestly sized living room with a window looking out onto the garden. There is a grey cloth sofa with two matching chairs set around a light wood centre table. A plain black square table with four matching chairs is squashed near the window. The only other furniture is a light wood TV stand with a black TV on it and a matching bookcase. However, what pulls me into the living room is what I see on the walls.

There are photos almost everywhere I look, and many of the photos are of me!

The photos make me feel a bit strange. I sit on the nearest chair and stare. Since Mummy was not there when most of these photos were taken, Nana or Auntie Cissy must have sent them to her. I didn't know that they were doing that. It makes me think of what Nana kept telling me — which I didn't always believe — that I meant the world to Mummy. Yet sitting here looking at the number of photos of me on the wall, it seems Nana may have had a point.

There are photos of Nana, Auntie Cissy, and Ama too, but there is none of Mummy. Disappointingly, there are also no photos of any men — no-one I can look at and wonder if he is my father, but I suppose there is no surprise there.

"Cissy has been sending me photos ever since I left Ghana," Mummy says behind me.

I turn to see her standing in the doorway.

18

"She started doing it without me even asking. It was very considerate, but then she has always been a thoughtful big sis," Mummy continues. "I put the photos up because they made me feel close to you, even though you were far away. Anyway, come, let me show you your bedroom."

Feeling unsure of what to make of what Mummy had just said, I stand and follow her out, wondering what my room will be like.

5

I wake with a start. An unfamiliar, woolly, brown blanket is covering me. For a minute, I don't know where I am, but then I remember.

I'm lying in bed in my new bedroom in Mummy's flat.

I look around the white-walled room which smells a little musty. There is a sink in the corner by the window that faces the back. The frame of the soft bed I'm lying on is a dark wood, as is the chest of drawers and wardrobe. Much needed colour is added to the room by the pink bedding and curtains.

The room doesn't feel like mine at all.

The bedroom that Ama and I shared in Nana's house was jam-packed with furniture, suitcases, and toys and I loved it. It was where Ama and I played and chatted late into the night when we were supposed to be asleep. When I moved into Nana's house, the bedroom was Ama's. She'd moved in when she was two. When Aunty Cissy's husband died suddenly, Aunty Cissy had moved back in with Nana as she wasn't coping well looking after Ama and continuing to hold down her full-time job as a teacher.

So, since the age of four when Mummy and I moved to Nana's house, Ama and I have shared a room. Like sisters.

This bedroom reminds me that life in London means life without Ama. That just feels so unfair!

My eyes filling with tears, I get up to look in my rucksack for a tissue. Honestly, I'm turning into such a crybaby. I never used to cry this much.

As I reach for my rucksack, I catch sight of my watch.

15.00

My goodness! How could I have slept for so long? The last thing I remember is lying down on the bed, waiting for Mummy as she went to the kitchen with the *kenkey* and *shito* I'd given her. She was going to fix breakfast. Oh no! That means I didn't eat the breakfast she made or lunch for that matter. As if on cue, my tummy starts to rumble. I'll freshen up, then go and find Mummy. I walk over to my two suitcases, which are against the wall by the window.

As I approach the window, I spot a furry animal darting up a tall tree in the garden. I lift up the white lace curtain to have a better look at the animal with a bushy tail. Wow, it is a grey squirrel! Leaning on the window sill, I stare at it. I've seen squirrels in photos before, but never in real life. I've *got* to tell Ama about this. Disappointingly, the squirrel moves and is soon hidden behind leaves. Though I stay by the window wishing the squirrel would reappear, it doesn't.

I'm about to step away from the window when I notice that in the garden there are two swings and, on one of the swings, a boy in a blue tracksuit is sitting with his headphones on. He is focused on something he is holding in his hands. I look closer and realise that he is playing an electronic game. Just then, he looks up at me. Embarrassed to have been caught staring at him, I give him an apologetic smile, but he doesn't smile back. He just stares at me with a frown before looking back down at his game. I step away from the window and let the curtain fall down. Well, that was awkward!

Kneeling in front of my suitcases, I open the smaller one to pull out my wash bag. I stand and move to the sink, catching sight of myself in the silver framed mirror above it. Heh! I look such a mess. My hair hasn't been combed since I left Nana's house and it shows. I have white marks around my eyes and my mouth from my sleep. No wonder the boy was staring at me and frowning. I feel even more embarrassed now. I hope I don't have to see him anytime soon.

I give my face a good wash before drying it with the towel Mummy left by the sink. I start to brush my teeth. As I brush, I look at myself in the mirror. My face is not exactly beautiful—it is too round and my cheeks too full. It probably doesn't help that I prefer my hair short. Nana Nancy often said that I had a wise soul and that this was reflected in my face. I think she was just telling me that I looked and acted older than my age, but I don't mind that.

After putting my toothbrush away, I cream my face before spraying and combing my hair. I could do with using the bathroom but at least I look better. Time to find Mummy and then the bathroom.

6

Mummy and I sit opposite each other eating yam, fish, and kontomire stew at her dining table. I'm famished and the food is hitting the spot. It's just after five in the evening, but sunlight is blazing through the window with no sign of sunset. I've changed into jeans and a red top after a warm bath in the beige bathroom next to Mummy's bedroom.

"I see you're enjoying the food, Esi," Mummy says.

With my mouth full of food, I nod. Mummy's food is almost as good as Nana's cooking.

"Remember I mentioned that my landlady Comfort lives downstairs?" Mummy says. "When you were asleep, she came to see if you had arrived safely and brought us this food. Comfort loves to cook. She is often bringing me food, which is handy as cooking isn't my thing."

Huh! I'd just assumed that Mummy had cooked the food we were eating. Surprised, I chew more slowly as I digest what she's said. This Comfort lady must be Mummy's friend as well as her landlady because I cannot imagine many landladies bringing their tenants food. Not that I know much about landladies. I wonder if that boy in the garden is related to Mummy's landlady.

I'm a little shocked that I didn't know that Mummy didn't like cooking. How come I didn't know? But then it's been many years since Mummy cooked for me and the two times she visited Ghana after her move, Nana made such a big fuss about Mummy relaxing that I assumed that was the reason why she never went into the kitchen. It is odd that Mummy doesn't like cooking when food is everything in Nana's house.

"How come you don't like cooking?" The thought escapes through my mouth before I can stop it. I still myself, not sure if Mummy will find my question impertinent.

"I blame Mama for that," Mummy says with a small smile. "She was always going on and on when I cooked, that in the end, I just didn't enjoy cooking."

Remembering how Nana was with Ama and me, I say, "She makes a fuss about everybody's cooking. Two years ago, she insisted that Ama and I start cooking so she started teaching us and has definitely been hard to please." But it hasn't put me off cooking.

"Mama told me that she was teaching you to cook," Mummy says with a smile. "She did the same with Cissy and me when we were children. Cissy grew to love cooking, but I didn't."

"You don't cook at all?" I ask, wondering how we'll eat. Will I have to do all the cooking? I don't like the idea of that.

"Yes, I do cook a little, but now that you are here, you'll have to do some too," Mummy says, making my heart sink.

"How often?" I ask.

Mummy sighs and her shoulders seem to drop. "My job is demanding, Esi. By the time I get home, I'm exhausted and, to be perfectly honest, the last thing I want to do is cook. So you'll probably do the cooking during the week and at the weekend, I'll cook."

I continue to eat quietly, dreading what Mummy has just said. That is far more cooking than I was doing in Ghana. How is it fair for me to do so much? Aren't Mummies supposed to cook for their children?

24

"You will also have to help with the housework," Mummy continues. "This is London, Esi. Here, there is no house help. It is just the two of us, so we both have to do our bit. You will be responsible for cleaning the bathroom, vacuuming the flat every weekend, and washing up."

I put my cutlery down. Suddenly, I'm not so hungry anymore. At Nana's house, once in a while, Ama and I helped Irene, Nana's house help, to sweep, tidy up, or wash up. We were also responsible for tidying up our own room. That I could cope with. But the cooking and chores Mummy is asking me to do sounds excessive. And unfair! If Mummy's work means she can't look after me, then why did she want me to come and live with her in London? I could still be living with Nana not having to do all this stuff.

With my appetite gone, I wonder if I can get up and leave now. I might as well get on with the washing up that I have to do.

"Tomorrow we'll go shopping," Mummy suddenly announces before I can excuse myself from the table. "I have to get the rest of your things for school."

After depressing me with all the cooking and housework that I've to do, now Mummy is reminding me about my new school which I'd much rather not think about. If she is setting out to make me feel down on my first evening in London, she is doing a good job.

"Are you excited about starting Hayes Road Secondary?" she asks expectantly.

I shrug. I really don't feel like talking.

In Ghana, the little she told me on the phone about Hayes Road school made me think that it was going to be nothing like Tesano International, the school Ama and I attended and where Auntie Cissy worked. I loved Tesano International and if I had any say in the matter, I would still be going there now. But I know I can't tell Mummy that. So it's easier just to say nothing.

"Before we go shopping tomorrow," Mummy continues, "We'll stop and say hello to Comfort. Then you can meet her son, Kojo. He'll be in your year at Hayes Road Secondary. It'll be good for you to meet him so that you have at least one familiar face when you start on Monday."

Oh no! Kojo must be the boy in the garden. It's going to be so embarrassing meeting him tomorrow.

I look up to see Mummy watching me intently.

"I'm so happy you're here, Esi," she says. "This is what I've been praying for since I arrived in London."

I smile, but don't say anything. I am happy that she is happy that I am here, but I know that I would happily be back in Ghana. Ghana is home, and this definitely doesn't feel like home. Is that how Mummy felt when she first moved here? I don't know why that thought has popped into my head, but now that it's there, I feel curious enough to ask, "How did you find London when you first came?"

Mummy is silent for a while as she stops eating and puts down her cutlery. "When I arrived in London, I came with five other nurses who had been hired in Ghana by the same recruitment agency. The agency had warned us to dress warmly and I thought I had, but I can remember to this day just how cold I felt when I arrived at Heathrow."

I nod, knowing exactly what she means.

"Luckily someone from the agency came to meet us with a minibus so we didn't have to find our own way from the airport. My mate Florence and I were taken straight to Middlesex Hospital where we had both been recruited to work as staff nurses. The others were taken to the private nursing homes where they were going to work." Mummy, looks lost in thought, as she twirls her glass of water round and round.

"At Middlesex Hospital, Florence and I were given nurses' accommodation near the hospital, but not together. I was offered a room with an ensuite in a shared four bedroomed flat with three other nurses—Dova from South Africa, Mary from the Philippines, and Sade from Nigeria."

"What was that like – sharing a flat with three strangers?" I ask, intrigued.

"Good, actually. Being new to this country, sharing a flat helped me a lot. My flatmates were friendly, and they became the people I would go to for information and advice. I learnt a lot from them about how things were at the hospital. They helped me adjust to living in London and overcoming my homesickness."

"You were homesick?" I gasp in surprise.

"Of course. I was without you for the first time, Esi. I was in a different country, thousands of miles away from my child. I longed to be with you. I had to rely on Nana and Cissy's updates to know what was happening to you. Even when I spoke to you on the phone, after a few minutes, you would say 'bye' and rush off to whatever you were doing before I called. It took a long time for me to get used to being here on my own without you."

This revelation leaves me stumped. It never occurred to me that Mummy felt homesick. In fact, I'd never thought about how Mummy felt about being away from me. Now I feel guilty. After Mummy left for London, because of Nana, Ama, and Auntie Cissy, I quickly got used to her being away and was quite content.

"What kept me going was that the income I was earning was allowing me to send money home to give you a decent education and pay for your upkeep," Mummy says. "My income also meant that I was able to help Nana financially."

Mummy pauses, looking down again at her glass. "That was the other good thing about living with my flatmates. Because they were immigrant nurses, we were going through similar experiences, so we understood each other. For instance, they were also sending money to their families in their countries."

"Did they have children, too?"

"Two of them did. Mary had three children in the Philippines who lived with her husband and Dova had two children who lived in South Africa with her mother. Sade didn't have any children but was supporting her parents in Nigeria."

"Are you still in contact with them?"

"Mary actually moved to the US to work last year because she thought that she could earn more money there. I don't hear from her so much, but Dova and Sade still work at Middlesex Hospital, so I see them regularly and they still share the staff flat."

Mummy carries on recounting the highs and lows of her experiences working in London. Though she was an experienced nurse in Ghana, soon after her arrival, she had to complete something called a Supervised Practice Course which she had to pay for herself before she could work as a nurse here.

"It was only when I started work that I realised that I'd been put on the lowest grade for a staff nurse, like many of the other African nurses I met at the hospital," Mummy says quietly. "The painful thing is that I know that staff nurses who joined from places like Australia or New Zealand were put on higher grades and paid more straight away. It made me feel that I was less valued than they were."

Though I don't know anything about nurses' grades, Mummy's last comment makes me feel bad for her. I wouldn't like it if someone was paid more than me because they came from a different country. That's just unfair.

"In spite of that, I knuckled down and tried to make the best of the opportunity that I'd been given," Mummy says brightly. "I did as much overtime as I could so that I could make as much money as possible in order to have money to live on as well as money to send home and save. That is how I managed to save the money to be able to move out of staff accommodation into this rented flat once I knew that I would be able to bring you ..."

The phone ringing interrupts Mummy. She gets up and picks up the phone on the top shelf of the bookcase.

"Good evening, Mama," she says. "Yes, Esi is awake. Hold on. I will give her the phone."

I take the phone excitedly. "Hello, Nana."

7

Standing at the sink in Mummy's kitchen washing up, I'm glad I got to speak to Nana. Her voice is as comforting over the phone as it is in person. I'm disappointed that Ama and Auntie Cissy were out, but Nana said that on Sunday she'll call again and I'll be able to speak to them. I'm looking forward to that.

Mummy's revelations this evening have been going round and round in my head. How come she never told me any of these things when I was in Ghana? Knowing some of what she has experienced since moving to London makes me feel like I know her a bit better. She is definitely brave. To come here by herself with no one to support her and deal with all the things she's dealt with takes guts. I'm not sure that I could do it or would want to do it.

"Oh good, Esi, you're washing up," says Mummy, as she walks into the kitchen. She must have finished her conversation with Nana. "Tell you what, I'll dry and put things away, so you can see where everything goes."

"Okay," I say, feeling more amenable to being helpful now that I know more about what she's been through.

Mummy picks up a tea towel from the hook by the door and starts drying things before putting them away. We work in companionable silence for a while and I start to think that maybe living with Mummy is not going to be so bad after all.

I wonder if this is a good time to ask Mummy about my father. She has talked a lot this evening, so maybe she might be willing to talk about my father as well.

As I wash the last dish in the sink, I clear my throat. "Mummy, I'd like to know more about my father."

Mummy stops what she's doing and frowns.

"Why are you asking me this now, Esi?" She shakes out the towel abruptly and it cracks the air.

I press on, even though I can sense it isn't going well. "I've always wanted to know more about him, Mummy. But when I've tried to talk to you in the past about him, you've always refused to tell me anything."

"Well, that's because I don't want to talk about him," Mummy snaps.

"But that's not fair, Mummy," I protest. "I have the right to know about my own father!"

"Your father has played no part in your life since you were four. He doesn't matter. Many people live life perfectly well without their fathers. My father died when I was very young and Mama raised me and Cissy by herself. *I* have not missed not having a father."

"But that is you, Mummy. I would like to know my father." I motion at her, pleading, and soap suds fall to the kitchen floor from my hands.

"Esi, why are you being so argumentative?"

"Mummy, I don't even know what my own father looks like. I don't know whether he is dead or alive. How is that right?" How can she not understand why I need to know about my father?

Mummy says nothing for a while, busying herself putting things away in the kitchen cupboards. Frustrated, I just stare at her.

31

Finally, she stops what she's doing and turns to me.

"Your father's name is Solomon Addo and he is alive," she says. "That's it. I'm not saying anymore about him."

I'm stunned. That is more than she's ever told me before.

Ecstatic, I say, "Thank you, Mummy."

As I get ready for bed, I mull over his name and the little burst of hope that I felt on the plane returns. I've learnt a bit more about my father, and it's only my first day in London. Maybe with time, I can get Mummy to tell me even more. I go to bed feeling more positive than before about being here with Mummy.

8

Count your blessings, name them one by one,
Count your blessings, see what God hath done!
Count your blessings, name them one by one ...

Praise and worship is in full swing when Mummy and I arrive at Anointed International Church. The red brick building, close to the paved shopping area with the bandstand-like enclosure, is unremarkable on the outside, but inside, the large hall is packed with an animated congregation whose singing is being led by a lively choir and five-piece band on stage.

Positioned by the door into the hall, an usher is handing out hymn books and service sheets.

"Sister Maggie, it is wonderful to see you this morning," he says enthusiastically when he sees Mummy. "I hope you are keeping well. Now who is this young lady?" he asks, his gaze on me.

"Brother Mike, this is my daughter, Esi," Mummy says. "She has just arrived from Ghana. She is going to be living with me now."

"Oh praise God. I didn't know you had a child, Sister Maggie," says Brother Mike, shaking my hand energetically. "Esi, you are very welcome to Anointed International."

I smile at him politely though my mind is whirling. How come he didn't know Mummy had a child? Has Mummy not talked about me? Why?

"Thank you, Brother Mike," Mummy says, before gently guiding me into the hall.

As we make our way through the packed congregation looking for somewhere to sit, a few people greet Mummy and look questioningly at me, making me wonder if Mummy has told *anyone* at church about me. Finally, we find two vacant seats next to each other. We stand and join in the singing, reading the words on the large monitor at the front of the hall.

I like church.

With Nana an elder at Tesano Methodist church, Sunday and church have always gone together. Every Sunday, I would put on one of my best dresses to go to church and that is what I have done today. I'm wearing a blue and white polka dot dress and my white flat shoes. Mummy is dressed more like she used to in Ghana, in a fitted purple batik dress and black heeled shoes. She is even wearing makeup today which suits her.

In Ghana, part of the fun of going to church was catching up with friends. Ama and I knew most of the children at church because we'd grown up with them. I wonder if I will make friends like that here? At the moment, that is hard to imagine.

A few rows ahead, a tall, slender woman catches my eye. Her long turquoise *bubu* and matching head tie look regal. As she turns to speak to the man with tortoiseshell glasses next to her, I recognise her. She is Mummy's landlady, Auntie Comfort. I met her yesterday before Mummy took me on the bus to an enormous supermarket to buy the rest of my school uniform and the other things she thought I needed like jumpers, trousers, a pair of brown boots and another black coat with a hood that was much warmer than the one Nana gave me. It felt nice that Mummy was buying me lots of new things, but buying clothes, school uniform and shoes from a supermarket was a first for me. I'd never come across that in Ghana before.

I wonder if the man Auntie Comfort is talking to is her husband. He was out when Mummy and I went to her flat yesterday. I notice the boy on the other side of Auntie Comfort. That must be Kojo. I'm not sure about that boy. He is not friendly at all. Yesterday, he barely said two words to me and when his mother suggested he walk with me to and from school, he looked angrily at her before putting his headphones on and walking off. I thought that was quite rude. I know he saw me through the window not looking my best, but still, I'm not so bad.

I wouldn't bother with Kojo but the idea of walking to and from school by myself is a little scary. It is yet another thing about London life that I'm not too happy about. In Ghana, I barely walked anywhere, never mind walking to school. In fact, nobody I knew walked to school. We were all driven there and back.

I'm relieved that Auntie Comfort and Mummy went ahead and agreed that Kojo should walk with me, even though he was clearly not happy about it. At least I won't get lost. Hayes is still so new to me. Mummy says she is going to show me the way to school by walking me there on my first day and walking me back at the end of the day. After that, she thinks I should know the way. I'm not convinced.

Give me joy in my heart, keep me praising.

The choir starts singing one of my favourite hymns. I join in and clap along with the rest of the congregation.

Give me joy in my heart, I pray,
Give me joy in my heart, keep me praising,
Keep me praising 'till the break of day.

When the hymn ends, the congregation is invited to sit down by a white, brown-haired man in a smart black suit and burgundy tie who walks on stage as the musicians and choir leave the stage.

The man, who introduces himself as Pastor Timothy, has a bellowing way of speaking and a tendency to say, "Can I hear an Amen?" every so often.

After telling the congregation about the planned events for the week, he says, "Sister Miriam is now going to read the first Bible lesson."

Sister Miriam, an elderly black woman dressed in a smart green dress with matching shoes and an elaborate hat, walks gingerly onto the stage and up to the microphone.

"The reading is taken from Psalm 103:2-4," Sister Miriam begins with a distinct Caribbean lilt.

Bless the Lord O my soul,

And forget not all His benefits:

Who forgives all your iniquities,

Who heals all your diseases,

Who redeems your life from destruction,

Who crowns you with loving kindness and tender mercies.

Here ends the word of the Lord.

"Amen," the congregation responds in unison.

"Thank you, Sister Miriam, for that beautiful reading," says Pastor Timothy before launching into a talk to the children about being grateful and counting our blessings. By the time, he ends with a prayer, I wonder if God has just sent me a message as I've not exactly been counting my blessings about moving to London.

The pastor dispatches the younger children to Sunday school and the older children to Youth fellowship.

Suddenly feeling nervous about being with a bunch of children I don't know, I say, "I will just stay here, Mummy."

"No Esi, you are going to Youth fellowship," Mummy replies firmly. "Look, there is Kojo. Follow him."

Reluctantly, I get up and follow Kojo and the other children as they head out through a side door. We walk down a corridor that leads to a set of stairs. Once up the stairs, the younger children turn right and the older children, including Kojo, turn left and enter a room ahead. The room is painted light blue with black chairs set around a large wooden table. The children are welcomed into the room by a black, older woman wearing a pink, old-fashioned dress. As I enter the room, she says, "Hello, I have not seen you before."

"This is my first time here," I say. When I start speaking, Kojo turns in his seat and glances at me before turning away again.

"You are very welcome," the woman continues. "I am Ms Mary. What is your name, my dear?"

"Esi Addo."

"Oh," Ms Mary says, looking at me more closely. "You remind me of someone. Who are your parents?"

"My mother is Maggie Addo," I reply. "I am here with her."

"I see," Ms Mary says pensively. "What about your father? What is his name?"

"My father is Solomon Addo," I say, my newly learnt information coming in handy. "But I live with ..."

"I knew it!" Ms Mary exclaims. "I know your father."

I stare at her. "You know my father?" I repeat as my body starts to shake. Ms Mary is the first person I've met who knows my father apart from Mummy, Nana and Auntie Cissy, and they won't tell me about him.

"Yes," Ms Mary continues. "I also know your grandmother. You look a lot like her."

"I look like Nana Nancy?" No one has ever said that to me before.

"No." Ms Mary shakes her head. "I mean your father's mother, Asantewa."

I stare at her in stunned silence as I continue to shake.

"Are you alright?" Ms Mary asks, looking concerned.

I nod but continue to stand and stare. Can this really be happening? All these years I have been wanting to know more about my father. Now, on my first day at this new church in London, I've met someone who can tell me not only about my father, but also about his mother, the grandmother that I'm named after, but know nothing about. This must be divine intervention.

My mind races with questions, but before I can ask any, I'm ushered along by another teacher to a seat.

Reeling from my encounter with Ms Mary, I pay no attention to Kojo on the other side of the table and barely follow what happens during the Youth fellowship. At the end, Ms Mary leads us to the church refreshment area to wait for our parents. When we get there, Kojo and some other boys huddle together talking. I stay near Ms Mary, wondering how I can get her to tell me more about my father.

But then I hear, "Esi." Mummy has entered the refreshment area and is walking towards me.

Ms Mary fixes her gaze on Mummy. "Hello," she says to her with her hand extended, as Mummy comes to a stop in front of me.

Mummy politely shakes her hand.

"I am Mary Ofori," Ms Mary says to Mummy. "I lead the Youth fellowship."

"Oh, I see." Mummy smiles at her. "I am Maggie Addo, Esi's mother."

"I have seen you at church a few times, but I didn't realise that you were Solomon's wife," Ms Mary continues, and the smile fades from Mummy's face. "But then I only met you once a long time ago in Ghana. I am a childhood friend of Asantewa. I have known Solomon since he was a baby."

My mind works overtime, as I wonder why Ms Mary is referring to Mummy as my father's wife? Mummy and Father aren't still married, are they?

Mummy stays silent, but her tense expression makes me wonder.

"I must say that Esi looks very much like Asantewa," Ms Mary carries on, as she smoothens her dress and fixes her eyes on Mummy.

"We have to go now," Mummy says abruptly, grabbing my hand. "It was nice to meet you."

"It was nice to meet you too, but ... how come you live here when Solomon is in Ghana?" Ms Mary asks, looking puzzled.

"Have a good day." Mummy ignores Ms Mary's question as she pulls me away, clearly keen to leave.

39

"See you next Sunday," Ms Mary calls out after us.

Mummy has an odd expression on her face as she leads me quickly out of church, only pausing briefly to wave and smile at Auntie Comfort and her husband.

All the way back to the flat on the bus, she is quiet and moody, clearly preoccupied by her encounter with Ms Mary.

Honestly, Mummy is baffling.

9

The sound of rain wakes me up. Sunlight is peeking through the gaps in the bedroom curtains.

Groggy, I squint at my watch on the bedside table.

7.00 am. Already?

I feel like I've barely slept, but I know it's time to get up as, this morning, I'm starting at Hayes Road School.

I cannot say I'm looking forward to it. In fact, I'm dreading it. As if that's not enough to contend with, it sounds like I'll be walking there in the rain. With a groan, I bury my head in the pillow, wishing I could just go back to sleep and forget about starting school and yesterday's events.

Yesterday, when we got back to the flat after church, Mummy was still moody. Auntie Comfort turned up a bit later with a pot of food, wondering why we'd rushed out of church, but Mummy only spoke to her briefly in the hall, making some excuse about not feeling very well. It appeared that she'd really been affected by what Ms Mary said to her. But why? That bit wasn't clear to me. I had so many questions I wanted to ask her, yet I didn't want her to get angry with me.

But in the evening, as we sat eating Auntie Comfort's *waakye* and beef stew for dinner, I couldn't stop myself asking, "Mummy, are you still married to my father?"

41

She started to frown. "Esi, don't start with your questions," she said.

"I have only asked you one question."

"Well, I'm not answering it," she snapped.

"Why not?" I asked.

"Because I don't want to talk about it. I'm the adult here, Esi. You can't order me to tell you things when I don't want to."

"But is it too much for me to know whether my own parents are married or not?" I asked, exasperated.

"Esi, be quiet and eat your food," Mummy replied. "I said I don't want to talk about it and that is that."

Fuming, I shut up and we continued to eat in silence.

It was a relief when Nana called and I was able to speak to Aunty Cissy and Ama. But talking to them made me miss them and my life in Ghana so much that it made me cry. I then felt frustrated that I couldn't speak to Ama the way I wanted to because Mummy was in the same room.

When I got off the phone, Mummy stood near me frowning. "Why were you crying, Esi?" she asked. "You're acting like you are not happy to be here."

Although there was more than a little truth in what she'd said, I shrugged and said nothing.

"Some people don't have mothers and wished they did," Mummy said. "You have a mother, you should be happy to be here with me."

Mummy went on, but I stopped listening. I didn't want to be lectured at by Mummy when she wasn't making any effort to see things from my perspective, especially about my father. And how can she not see that I am simply homesick, especially when she herself was homesick when she first arrived in London. I cut her off, saying, "Yes, Mummy." To change the subject, I said, "I will clear the table now and wash up."

That took the wind out of her sails. Thankfully, she sat down on the sofa and put the TV on as I cleared the table and went to wash up in the kitchen. When I finished in the kitchen, I quickly used the bathroom before quietly slipping into my bedroom and going to bed early so as to avoid spending any more time with her.

But sleep evaded me. I tossed and turned, mulling things over in my head. What could have happened between Mummy and my father that, all these years later, she still couldn't bring herself to talk about him? Could they still be married? Why would they still be married when they'd been living apart for so long? But then, I couldn't recall having been told that Mummy and Father were divorced. So maybe they weren't. It was so annoying not knowing these things about my own parents.

Thoughts of why Father hadn't come to see me and the bitter feeling that always accompanied those thoughts plagued me. That kept me awake long into the night until I finally fell into an exhausted sleep.

Loud knocking on my bedroom door makes me jump.

"Esi, are you awake?" Mummy calls out from behind the door.

"Yes, Mummy." I know I can't put off getting out of bed any longer.

"Good. Start getting dressed, please."

43

"Alright," I say, forcing myself out of bed.

Half an hour later, I'm dressed and standing in front of the silver mirror in my room. I spray my hair with detangling spray before starting to comb it out. As I do, my anxiety about the day ahead intensifies as I stare at myself in the unfamiliar white blouse, grey skirt, and red blazer with the Hayes Road School logo on it.

There is another knock on the door. I put my afro comb down and open the door. Mummy is standing there in a pair of blue jeans and a white short-sleeved lace blouse.

"Oh Esi, you look so smart," she exclaims, looking much happier than she did yesterday. "C'mon, let's eat some breakfast. We have about half an hour before we have to leave."

Twenty minutes later, we are in the hall in our coats and Mummy is holding my hands as she prays.

"*Nyame, hwe Esi ma me.* God, look after Esi as she starts her new school. Keep blessing her over the months and years to come. There is nothing she cannot overcome with your grace. In Jesus name, Amen," she says, much like Nana would.

My hands freed, I open the front door and we step out of the flat with our hoods on. The sky is grey, but the rain is subsiding, which is a relief. It is also a relief that there is no sign of Kojo. Tomorrow, I have to walk to school with him, but this morning, already feeling anxious, I can do without his unfriendliness. Mummy and I stroll down the road before turning onto a street with a small parade of shops. At the end of the street, the clouds start to lift revealing blue sky. "The school is not too far now," Mummy says, as she leads me onto a busier road.

I nod as I look around. There are other children wearing the Hayes Road School uniform walking too. Though some of them are walking with an adult, most are walking on their own. Some

44

emerge from the flats and houses that line the road. Hayes Road School is clearly a school for local children. That wasn't true of Tesano International. Most of the pupils there didn't live in Tesano but travelled in from all over Accra.

"There is the school," Mummy suddenly says.

We are nearing a long, short wall with metal railings above it. Behind it is a tall, brown, four storey building with its car park to one side and gated sports field to the other. There is a small green garden to the front with a paved pathway and a large sign with *Hayes Road Secondary school* printed on it. There is nothing particularly welcoming about the school. I wonder what made Mummy choose this school for me? She has never actually told me that.

Feeling anxious once again, I follow Mummy as she walks towards the door signposted *Main reception*.

10

I've been shown rooms, walked up and down stairs as well as corridors. But everything is a blur and I'm struggling to remember anything. Mummy waved me goodbye about fifteen minutes ago in the school reception. Now I'm being shown around the school by Mrs Pier, the head of year nine, a slight, grey-haired woman in a flowery dress who has been talking virtually nonstop.

"Well, Essie, these are the year nine form rooms," Mrs Pier explains, as she comes to a standstill on the third-floor corridor that we've been walking down.

Mrs Pier has been saying my name in that odd way since we met downstairs. Mummy and I both repeated my name correctly to her, but still, she continued to say Essie. I don't understand why.

Mrs Pier walks to a door marked 9H and says, "This will be your form room." I don't even get a chance to gather myself before she knocks and opens the door.

The classroom is large and sunlit with two windows looking out onto the school sports field. The year nine pupils are sat in pairs behind wooden desks facing the front of the class. All eyes seem to turn and fix on me as I walk in, making me very self-conscious. Mrs Pier leads me to the tall bearded man standing by the whiteboard.

"Mr Herbert, this is Essie, who is starting in your class today," Mrs Pier says in a loud voice.

Mr Herbert smiles and shakes my hand as he booms, "Hello Essie, I've been expecting you."

What! Now he is also saying my name in that strange way!

"Essie, I leave you in Mr Herbert's capable hands," Mrs Pier says with a smile before leaving the room.

"Essie, you are very welcome to 9H," says Mr Herbert. "You'll find us a very friendly bunch...."

But I'm not really listening to him. I'm wondering how to tell him that my name is not Essie. Otherwise, he'll be calling me that every day and that will be very annoying!

"Mr Herbert, my name is pronounced Esi," I blurt out, enunciating the sound of each letter.

"Oh, sorry. Let me try again. Essi? Is that better?"

I suppose it is better, so I nod, though I'm still baffled as to why he can't just say my name correctly.

"Essi, you are going to sit here," Mr Herbert says, as he walks me to a seat next to a girl with blonde hair in a long ponytail. As I sit down, the girl flashes me a confident smile and says, "Hiya, I'm Lisa."

I smile back.

"Lisa will be your buddy," Mr Herbert says. "She'll keep an eye on you and help you find your way around the school."

I notice that Lisa's eyebrows look like they've been plucked, her lips are shiny as if she is wearing lip gloss and her skirt is halfway up her thighs. I'm surprised. At Tesano International, you would be sent to the head teacher's office if you came to school looking like that.

But Lisa is smiling at me and telling me, "We're going to be mates," so I put my reservations to one side.

Mr. Herbert says as he walks away, "Essi, you haven't missed much. We were still doing the register." He goes back to his desk near the whiteboard and starts calling out names to responses of, "Yes sir." When he says, "Kojo Adjei?" and Kojo gruffly replies, "Yes sir," I turn to look at Kojo. How had I not noticed him earlier?

Kojo nods at me from where he is sitting near the back of the room next to a boy with curly hair and a dark tan complexion. In his school uniform without his headphones on, he looks quite different. Is it going to be a good thing that he is in my form? I'm not sure. He still doesn't look very friendly.

11

Lisa is doing my head in. I've heard children using that phrase at school and it really fits how I'm feeling about Lisa.

On my first day, it quickly became clear that I had nothing in common with her. But, because Mr Herbert made Lisa my buddy, I haven't been able to get away from her. Her friends are just as bad. They all weirdly have the same hairstyle, socks, shoes and wear their uniform in the way that Lisa does. All they do is gossip about boys, clothes, and makeup, as well as how amazing Lisa is.

At Tesano International, Ama and I kept away from people like that. We preferred to laugh and tell jokes or talk about films, music and books. Luckily there were a lot of likeminded children in our class so we had a lot of friends.

I've been at Hayes Road for five days and every day, just like now, I daydream about being back at Tesano International with Ama. It's break time and I'm sitting in the sheltered outdoor seated area with Lisa and her mates. Suddenly, I feel my hair being touched. I jump up and Imogen, one of Lisa's friends, is standing right behind me.

"What are you doing?" I ask.

"Your hair is sooo cute. I just wanted to see what it felt like."

"Nonsense. How would you like it if I touched your hair without asking you first?"

"Chill, Essi. No need to get so worked up."

49

Still irritated, I bite my tongue, telling myself not to get into an argument with this girl. I sit down again.

"You're getting a bit hot under the collar, aren't you?" Lisa says. "What's the big deal?"

I scowl at her and don't bother to respond. How ignorant can you be not to know that you are invading someone's personal space by touching their hair without their permission!

"Lighten up, Essi," says Chloe, another of Lisa's friends. "Look, I learnt this cool dance move yesterday. Check this out."

She leaps up and starts doing some strange jumping and wriggling about in front of everyone in the sheltered area.

What is this girl doing? I think as I watch in amazement. The other girls cheer her on.

"Do they do this dance where you come from?" Chloe asks, a little breathless from her exertions.

"No," I say.

"Maybe you can teach us some of your dance moves. Black people are the best dancers," Chloe continues.

Doesn't this girl know that not all black people are the same? I tell her, "Actually, I don't like dancing," to make sure that I'm not asked to dance again.

"Oh shame," says Chloe. "We love dancing, don't we, Denise?"

"Yeah." Denise, another of Lisa's friends, gets up from her seat next to Lisa and starts doing some funny dancing with Chloe. Lisa and Imogen cheer them on as if they are doing something amazing. I'm mortified and even more so when I catch Kojo walking past with his friends; the boy he sits next to in our form room and a

50

small, pale, white girl who looks a little dishevelled with her brown hair in a long plait. They glance at me before looking at the dancing and starting to laugh. I just want to crawl into a hole.

Later after break, as we sit in Mr Burrell's history class, Lisa starts annoying me yet again. She keeps treating me like someone who cannot speak for herself. Mr Burrell splits us into small groups to discuss the topic he has put on the board. Every time I try to speak, Lisa jumps in and speaks over me. I keep scowling at her, but she takes no notice. Finally, I snap. "Lisa, I'm speaking now."

She looks startled. "Alright, Essi! Don't get your knickers in a twist."

I have no idea what that even means.

In fact, I've no idea why Lisa behaves the way she does towards me, but I sense she makes assumptions about me because I'm from Ghana and not the UK. Maybe I'm reading too much into it. I just wish I could get away from her!

12

I see Kojo approaching, deep in conversation with his two friends.

I've been waiting for him by the school gate, our agreed meeting point after school. I've been walking with him to and from school for two weeks now but he still rarely speaks to me. Yet I know he talks, so why doesn't he talk to me?

When Kojo and his friends reach me, he nods at me, but his friend, the tall, curly-haired boy who sits next to him, smiles at me and says, "Hi Esi, we've not met properly. I'm Mohammed."

"Hi," I say, pleased that he's talking to me.

"Hiya Esi," says Kojo's other friend, the girl with the long plait. "I'm Karen."

"Hi," I say, smiling back.

"Cool hair," she says, gazing at my short afro.

I manage to say, "Thanks," before she says, "Got to go. Mum's waiting for me. Bye."

"See you tomorrow," Kojo and Mohammed call out to her, as she dashes off in the direction of a white car parked near the school gate.

"How are you finding Hayes Road so far?" Mohammed asks, as his attention shifts back to me.

"So-so." I gesture with my hand.

He nods as if he understands.

"How is it going with Lisa?" he asks with a slight smile.

I make a face that makes him laugh. Even Kojo smiles.

"I know she's your buddy, but you don't have to stay with her all the time," Mohammed says. "Why don't you join us at break tomorrow?"

I glance at Kojo, not sure that he would want me to do that.

"Don't worry about Kojo," says Mohammed. "It takes him a while to get used to someone, but he's alright really."

Kojo jabs Mohammed with his elbow which only makes Mohammed laugh. Kojo looks at me then. "You're welcome to join us if you want," he says shyly, to my amazement.

"Okay, I will," I say immediately before he changes his mind. I'm so happy. Finally, I can get away from Lisa and her mates and hopefully make some new friends.

"Well, I'd better go," says Mohammed. "See you guys tomorrow."

"Laters, Mohammed," says Kojo as he and Mohammed do a fist bump.

I smile and wave before Kojo and I start walking home.

I'm keen for the usual silence not to return. So I start talking in the hope that Kojo will continue talking to me.

"How long have you, Mohammed, and Karen been friends?"

"We were friends at primary school." He kicks at a stone, making it jump ahead of us.

Thinking aloud, I say, "A lot of my friends in my last school I'd known since I started school."

"At what age?"

"Four years old."

"Wow! That's a long time. You must really miss them then." Kojo glances at me before looking back at the stone he's kicking.

"Yes, I do," I say with a shrug. But I don't want sadness to spoil my first proper conversation with Kojo so I keep talking.

"Have you always lived in Hayes?" I ask.

"I was born here. What about you?"

"I was born in Ghana. This is my first time out of Ghana."

"Things must seem quite strange then," Kojo says, his face softening.

"Yes, it does a bit." I don't tell him how strange it all is, and that I would love to be back in Ghana. I don't want him to think I'm a cry-baby.

"I've been to Ghana," he says, "but it was a long time ago. About six years."

"Where did you go to in Ghana?"

"We stayed in Achimota with my grandparents."

That makes me smile. I know Achimota. "I lived in Tesano with my grandma until I left Ghana. Do you know Tesano?"

"No, it doesn't ring a bell, but then, I don't know Ghana well. Did your father live with your grandma as well?" Kojo asks, after a moment.

There is an awkward silence as I think of what to say. Finally, not looking at him, I say, "No. I haven't seen my father since I was four years old. So, I don't remember him."

Kojo doesn't respond at first. "You don't remember anything about him?" he says finally, sounding incredulous.

"I know that I have his surname and that my middle name is his mother's name." It's stupid to feel ashamed of something I have no control over, but I can't help it.

There is silence again as I feel Kojo's gaze on me. I summon the courage to look at him.

"It must be tough not knowing your father," he says with sympathy in his eyes.

I nod but don't want to get morose in front of him. I move the conversation on.

"I haven't met your father yet," I say.

"He's out quite a lot. On weekdays, he leaves the house early and normally doesn't get home until after six-thirty."

"Do you get on with him?"

"Yeah. He's cool!" The warmth that lights up Kojo's angular face makes me instantly envious.

Wouldn't it be wonderful to have a father that I felt that way about? "Do you do a lot with him?" I find myself asking.

"Yes, we both really like music, so we listen to music together. We also like playing video games."

"So that explains the music I hear sometimes when I'm in the living room," I say, hoping I don't sound too envious.

"Oh, I hope it doesn't disturb you and your Mum," Kojo says apologetically.

"It's fine," I say truthfully.

Kojo and I continue to talk all the way home. I'm surprised by how much I warm to him, now that he is talking to me. As we near the flats, Kojo tells me about how Auntie Comfort is a hoarder. I'd already worked that out from the amount of stuff there is in their living room. When he mentions that Auntie Comfort keeps things she values in boxes under her bed, it makes me wonder if Mummy does the same. I haven't ventured into Mummy's room yet, but maybe it might be worth looking around to see what I can find about my father. But I dare not do it when Mummy is in the flat, so that means the only time I can do it is after school when Mummy is still at work.

Maybe I'll have a look today.

13

As we reach the flats, I come up with a reason why I cannot go to Auntie Comfort's flat today. All the other days since I started walking home with Kojo, I've always gone to Auntie Comfort's flat and remained there until Mummy returns from work. It would have been nice to go in with Kojo today now that we are getting on, but I'm keen to see what I can find in Mummy's room.

"I think I'll do my homework at home today," I say to Kojo.

Kojo looks surprised. "Okay, I'll tell Mum. See you in the morning."

"Yes, see you tomorrow," I say, feeling buoyed up.

I unlock the front door with my key and shut the door behind me. I run up the stairs and dump my school rucksack and coat on my bed before going to Mummy's room. The room is tidy but devoid of character. It could be anyone's room. I hurry to the white wardrobe and do a quick search, but there is nothing in there apart from clothes and shoes. I move to the bed and look under it. There are two cardboard boxes there. The first one I open contains official-looking letters, but the second box is full of photos, which is promising. I empty the photos onto the brown carpet.

My heart starts thumping when I spot a professional looking photo of a younger looking Mummy sitting with a baby, presumably me, with a man standing next to her with his arm around her. I know straight away that this is my father. I peer closely at his face. Confident eyes stare out of the dark, striking face framed by low cut hair. I can't tear my eyes away. Mummy and my father look happy. What could have gone so wrong that Mummy cannot bear to speak about him now?

I put the photo down and look through the other photos on the carpet to see what else I can find. There are photos of Mummy pregnant and looking content, more photos of her and my father looking in love, some of my father on his own, and one shot of him looking down at me as he carries me as a baby. The photo makes me cry but it also makes me mad. Mummy and my father, for whatever reason, messed up their marriage and because of that, I've been deprived of having a father in my life. That is so unfair! I use my sleeve to wipe away my tears. As I do, a white photo album catches my attention.

Opening it, on the first page is written, *The marriage of Solomon Addo and Maggie Jones 6th June 1985.*

Turning the page, a stunning photo of Mummy and my father dressed in matching white lace takes my breath away. I keep turning the pages. I spot photos of Nana and Auntie Cissy standing next to a bald, well-dressed man who I recognise from the photo next to Ama's bed as Auntie Cissy's husband. When I get to a photo of an older couple wearing expensive looking white lace outfits, I stop. They could be my father's parents because the man looks a bit like Father. With what Ms Mary said at church ringing in my ears, I get up with the photo and look at myself in the mirror, trying to see the resemblance between me and the woman in the photo. Her hair is short like mine and I guess I can see a little resemblance in our faces. But am I seeing it because I want to see it? I'm not sure.

Ring. Ring. The doorbell rings.

Oh no! Who can that be?

Mummy has her own key and she shouldn't be home now. It is only four thirty and she is normally home after six. I hurry to

Mummy's window and crane my neck to see who is at the front door. Only the top of the person is visible, but it's enough to know that Auntie Comfort is at the door. I'll have to open the door or she won't go away. Wiping away any tear marks from my face, I rush out of Mummy's room, carefully shutting the door behind me. The doorbell rings again as I run down the stairs to the front door.

When I open the door, a frowning Auntie Comfort, in a black knitted dress and a colourful beaded necklace, says, "Ah Esi, I was starting to get worried."

Thinking of an excuse, I say, "Sorry, I was in the bathroom."

"Hope you checked who it was before you opened the front door."

"Yes, Auntie, I did."

"I just wanted to see if you were alright. Kojo told me that you want to do your homework here today?"

"Yes, that's right."

"But, Esi, I don't think your mother wants you to be at home by yourself after school."

"I'm already in the middle of my homework, Auntie Comfort," I say quickly. "I promise that tomorrow I will come with Kojo to your place as normal."

"Alright, Esi. I'll see you tomorrow. Don't hesitate to come down if you need anything."

"Yes, Auntie Comfort," I say. "See you tomorrow."

As she walks away, I close the door, relieved, praying that God will forgive me for lying. I run back to Mummy's room and pack the photos in the box as neatly as possible. Spotting a smaller version of the professional photo of Mummy, my father and me as a baby, I decide to hold on to it, hoping Mummy won't notice. With everything back in the box, I push both boxes back under the bed. I make sure that everything looks like I found it before leaving the room. Back in my room, I hide the little photo in the small zipped compartment of my rucksack.

Thinking of what I'll say when Mummy returns from work and finds me in the flat instead of downstairs with Auntie Comfort, I go to the dining table to do my homework with my heart still pumping hard. But I struggle to concentrate on my homework. All I keep thinking about is my father's face. I'm so happy that I found Mummy's stash of photos. At least I now know what he looks like. It's something I've wanted to know for so long.

14

Hanging out with Kojo, Mohammed, and Karen is the best thing about being at Hayes Road Secondary.

Kojo, especially, has been a revelation. Five weeks in London and he is the one I feel most free with.

I'm talking less and less to Mummy. I haven't been able to speak to her about my issues with Lisa or how much I still miss my old life. Even with Father, we are back to her saying nothing about him. After finding the photos under her bed, I almost asked her that night if she had photos of my father just to see what she would say. But then I decided against it. I knew she would just get annoyed with me again.

Calls to Ghana are not frequent enough. Boredom is becoming more and more a feature of my life, especially at the weekend. Unlike at Nana's house, where at the weekend I would be out and about, doing things with Ama or in Nana's bakery, helping and giggling with Ama as we listened to Nana and her friends conversing; here I spend quite a lot of time in my room by myself.

Mummy and I never go to see anyone and no one comes to see us, apart from Auntie Comfort. Even with Auntie Comfort - Mummy's closest friend here from what I can see - Mummy often talks to her at the front door. Since the incident with Ms Mary, we've stopped going to church. Mummy says Anointed International is not the right church for us, but I know she just wants to avoid Ms Mary.

So, I thank God that I have Kojo to talk to.

This morning, as we walk to school, we're talking about books.

"Science fiction is the best," says Kojo.

"Really?" I laugh and shake my head. "Nah, I prefer dramas and books by people like Ama Ata Aidoo."

"Oh, I've read one of her books."

"You have? But she doesn't write science fiction!"

"I know," says Kojo with a chuckle. "But this summer holiday, I came across a box in the hall cupboard which hadn't been unpacked since we moved into the flat five years ago. I found some of Mum's books, and they included a few books by Ghanaian authors. *Anowa* by Ama Ata Aidoo was one of them. It looked interesting so I was intrigued and asked Mum if I could read it. She said okay. So I read it and actually enjoyed it."

"Well, I must say that I'm shocked."

"Why?"

"Because it's not science fiction, for a start. I read Anowa about a year ago, but most of my friends in Ghana haven't read it, so I didn't expect to meet anyone in London who'd read it."

"I'm a multifaceted guy, Esi," Kojo says, popping up his collar.

"Look at you with your big words," I say, laughing.

Our talk turns to TV.

I don't watch much TV in the flat with Mummy, but after school at Kojo's place, once we have done some homework, Auntie Comfort allows Kojo and I to watch TV and play music. So I now know some of the music and TV programmes that I hear being talked about at school, which makes me feel like a little less of an outsider. Kojo loves listening to RnB and hip-hop. I like some of the music he listens to but I've introduced him to Ghanaian highlife and hiplife, too. As yet, I have no favourite TV programmes as none of the TV programmes I watched in Ghana are shown here, so I watch the programmes that Kojo likes. His favourite programme, *Malcolm in the Middle,* is quite funny, so I don't mind watching it.

Going to Kojo's flat after school has meant that I've got to know his mum, Auntie Comfort. Though she works from home as a bookkeeper, she always seems to have a lot of time for Kojo and me, including cooking for us. I love her food. Eating at her flat every weekday has made up for Mummy's lack of culinary skills. She cooks everything from scratch, even making her own ice cream. When I go home with Mummy after she returns from work, I cook food for her but don't eat, as I've already eaten dinner with Kojo.

What I like the most about Auntie Comfort is how she is with Kojo. Every so often, she will give Kojo a kiss on the cheek or put her arms around him for no apparent reason. He will grumble, "Oh Mum," but will hug her back. If I'm honest with myself, I know that I would love it if Mummy and I had that kind of relationship.

But we don't. It's hard to imagine that we ever will and that's rather sad but I have no idea what can be done about it.

15

Since I started at Hayes Road School, I have been put in the bottom set for all my subjects.

Me! How? At Tesano International, I won prizes and was often top of my class. Here, it is like the school thinks I learnt nothing before I got here. It is so frustrating.

This morning, I am sitting in Maths. Lisa is next to me, getting up to her usual antics, trying to wind me up. Since I stopped hanging out with her and her mates, she has been making it her business to show me how unhappy she is with me 'dumping her and her friends,' as she puts it. Right now, I've more important things to worry about than her nonsense.

"It is likely that most of you in this set will do the foundational GCSE in maths," Mr Hersy has just announced.

I am incensed! How can I do the foundational GCSE where the highest grade you can get is a C? I am perfectly capable of doing the higher GCSE.

In English, after lunch, I decided to ask Miss Ashley about GCSEs. "Most of you are likely to do the foundational GCSE," she says as well, making my heart sink.

For the rest of the day, I am seething.

On the way back home, I complain to Kojo. He's in higher sets for all his subjects.

"Your Mum should go and speak to Mrs Pier," Kojo suggests. "My Mum has gone down to the school many times when she's been unhappy."

"But I'm not sure my mother will go," I grumble.

"Give her a chance. Speak to her about it," Kojo says.

So tonight, when I hand Mummy the tray with the chicken and rice dinner that I've cooked for her as she sits slumped in her blue nurse's uniform on the sofa, I decide to tell her about what happened at school. As she eats, she listens quietly to what I say.

"You have only just started at the school, Esi," she says when I finish talking. "Exercise patience. Things will work out."

"But Mummy, how long am I meant to exercise patience for? Won't you go and speak to Mrs Pier about it?" I say, disappointed by her response, as there is no sign of her being angry for me. "This is an important year when the GCSEs I'm going to take will be decided."

"It is only the first term, Esi. Your teachers are still assessing your level."

I remember then that on my last day at Tesano International, I was given an envelope to give to my new school by Mrs Ofori, my form teacher. It had all my reports in it as well as records of commendations and prizes that I had been given at school. I gave it to Mummy when I got here. What happened to it?

"Did you take in the envelope from Tesano International?" I ask.

"Yes." Mummy sets down her fork on the half-empty plate. "But the school did not accept it. They said they would make their own assessments."

"You didn't insist that they look at it?" I ask, incensed. "Maybe that is why I have been put in the bottom set."

"Watch how you speak to me, Esi." Mummy frowns. "Listen, your teachers know what they are doing. I'm sure they will move you up once they have finished their assessments."

"You don't know that, Mummy," I shout. She's not listening. I don't want to be in the bottom set. I am better than that.

"Don't shout at me, Esi," Mummy responds, her voice raised. "I am not going to tolerate insolence from you."

I keep my eyes down and don't speak. I'm not going to say sorry. I'm not.

"Go to your room," Mummy says angrily.

I walk off. *Some mother she is.*

I've put up with leaving Ghana when I didn't want to.

I've put up with her mood swings.

I've put up with her not wanting to talk about my father.

I have even put up with doing most of the house chores and the cooking.

Why can she not go to school and stand up for me? Isn't that what a mother is supposed to do?

Fuming, I slam my bedroom door shut and throw myself on my bed. How am I really benefiting from being here? Before I left Ghana, Nana, Auntie Cissy, and Mummy went on and on about how an English education is first class and that it will set me up for life. But the reality is that at Tesano International, I felt confident at school because I was being told by my teachers that I was bright and doing well. Here, at Hayes Road School, I'm starting to doubt myself. How exactly is that helping me?

If Mummy is not going to do anything to help, then maybe I am better off back in Ghana.

The thought has me sitting up, my heart racing.

Yes, if things don't improve, I will have to work out how to go back to Ghana. I'm sure Mummy will not be happy, but if she is not willing to fight for me, why should I stay here?

16

Kojo and I are watching *Malcolm in the Middle* when Auntie Comfort walks in from the kitchen.

"I wonder where your mother is?" she says with a slight frown.

The brass clock above the piano in their living room shows the time to be six forty-five. Mummy is normally here around six, so she is quite late.

"She didn't tell me she was going to be late," I say, not mentioning that I barely spoke to her this morning.

"I'll call her," Auntie Comfort says, walking to her black handbag hanging on the side of one of the dining chairs. Getting out her mobile phone, she dials Mummy's number. "Hmm, it's gone to voicemail. That's a bit strange. Well, hopefully, she'll be here soon."

"Should I go up to the flat and wait for her?" I ask, conscious that I've stayed longer than I would normally do.

"Oh no, there's no need for that. Just wait here," Auntie Comfort says with a smile before returning to the kitchen.

Kojo and I go back to watching our TV programme.

A few minutes later, I hear a key turning and the sound of the front door being opened. "Comfort, Kojo, *maadu*. I'm home," a man calls out.

Kojo gets up and walks into the hall, saying, "Hi, Dad. Mum's in the kitchen."

I've not met Kojo's Dad properly yet. He normally leaves for work before I arrive in the morning and does not return before Mummy picks me up in the evening.

"Hey, my little man," I hear him say. "How was school today?"

"Okay. Nothing exciting."

"That good, eh?" I hear Kojo's Dad reply, laughing.

As they step into the living room, I'm sitting awkwardly on the sofa, feeling a little nervous.

"Dad, this is Esi, Auntie Maggie's daughter," Kojo says as he glances at me.

"Oh yes, hello my dear, it is lovely to meet you properly at last." Kojo's Dad walks towards me, his hand outstretched. "Comfort and Kojo have told me a lot about you. I'm Kofi."

I stand up and shake his hand. "Hello, Uncle Kofi. It is nice to meet you, too."

Uncle Kofi sports a short afro, a bushy beard, and tortoiseshell glasses. He isn't very tall—Kojo is almost as tall as him. But despite that, his presence fills the room. The warmth of his smile makes me want to smile back at him.

"How are you finding Hayes Road School?" he asks me.

"Okay, I suppose."

"Wow, you sound as enthusiastic as Kojo," Uncle Kofi says, smiling.

"Good evening, dear. How was your day?" Auntie Comfort says as she walks in, holding two steaming plates of beans stew, fish, and fried plantain.

"Tiring," Uncle Kofi says as he gives Auntie Comfort a kiss on the cheek.

"Well, you can relax now. Dinner is ready."

"Wonderful." Uncle Kofi takes his black suit jacket off and leaves it on the sofa.

Auntie Comfort places the plates on the dining table before turning to Kojo and me. "You guys have already eaten, but if you fancy fried plantain," she says, "you are welcome to help yourself."

"Yes, please," Kojo and I respond almost in unison.

"I'll get more fried plantain from the kitchen then."

So, I find myself sitting at the dining table, enjoying fried plantain with Kojo whilst Uncle Kofi and Auntie Comfort eat their dinner.

"Esi, have you seen my Comfort special?" says Uncle Kofi. "Comfort doesn't feel she's fed me unless she has given me enough food to feed five people."

"You don't have to eat it all if it is too much," Auntie Comfort retorts.

"Eh, so you can complain to your mother that I don't eat your food after you've slaved in the kitchen. No please, I will eat it all. You know your mother already thinks you should have aimed higher when you married."

"Are you talking about the same woman who calls just to speak to you, her favourite son-in-law?" asks Auntie Comfort.

"Oh yes, that is true," Uncle Kofi says with a smile. "She does call to speak to me. What can I say? She has succumbed to my charms."

I smile as Kojo rolls his eyes.

As the evening progresses, I sit watching Kojo, Auntie Comfort, and Uncle Kofi talking, laughing and teasing each other. I don't say much, but I listen and laugh. I'm captivated by how Auntie Comfort and Uncle Kofi speak to each other and seem to find things to laugh about. It makes me conscious of the fact that I don't remember having seen this kind of exchange between husband and wife before. I've no recollection of exchanges between Mummy and my father, and Nana's home is full of females.

I wonder if Kojo knows how lucky he is to have a mother and father who clearly care a lot for each other and for him. I can't help feeling envious, but I try hard not to let it show.

"Gosh, it is nearly eight o'clock and your mother is still not here, Esi," Auntie Comfort says suddenly. "Let me try calling her once again." She digs in her bag and pulls her mobile phone out. She dials Mummy's number, then frowns as she says, "Hello? Who is this?"

"The police!" she cries, and my heart drops.

"I am Comfort Adjei, Maggie's friend. And her next of kin," Auntie Comfort adds hastily. "Is Maggie okay? ... Oh my goodness!"

Feeling really scared, I say, "What's happened?"

Auntie Comfort reaches out to hold my hand as she speaks into her phone. "Alright. I will be there as quickly as I can."

When she puts her phone down, she says, "I am really sorry Esi, but your mother has been hit by a car and has been taken to hospital."

Fear like I've never known takes over me. I hear myself screaming as everything starts to spin.

17

Accident and Emergency.

Not in Middlesex hospital, but in a hospital in Ealing. Auntie Comfort explained in the car that there had been no beds available for Mummy in Middlesex hospital.

So many people. Sitting. Waiting.

Uniformed staff rushing about.

Auntie Comfort stops a nurse. "We're here to see Maggie Addo. The police say she was brought here by ambulance."

"Are you family?" the nurse asks.

"I am her next of kin," Auntie Comfort says firmly. "I'm here with her daughter."

"Please come with me," the nurse tells us.

As we walk, the nurse explains that Mummy has been moved to ICU. I don't know what ICU means but Auntie Comfort's expression makes me worry.

After walking for a while, we get to the ward door signposted Intensive Care Unit. Now I understand. The nurse presses the buzzer and speaks into the intercom.

Soon Auntie Comfort and I are standing in ICU. "Maggie Addo is just being sedated," an ICU nurse tells us, "so if you wait here a moment, I'll check if it's okay for you to see her."

As we wait, Auntie Comfort puts her arm around me and rubs my shoulder in a reassuring way, but I can see that she is worried. I feel sick.

All the way to the hospital in Auntie Comfort's grey Honda, I prayed to God. Was he punishing me for being unhappy with Mummy and wanting to go back to Ghana? I prayed that if God helped Mummy recover, I would stop moaning about her.

The ICU nurse returns and tells us to follow her. We walk past hospital beds and curtained cubicles until we get to Mummy lying, eyes closed, on a trolley bed.

Tubes linked to a monitor are protruding from her left arm.

Beeping.

I stand staring at her, feeling so scared. "Is she just asleep?" I ask Auntie Comfort.

"Yes, Esi, she's asleep because of the sedation."

Auntie Comfort rubs my back reassuringly before approaching the doctor standing next to Mummy's bed. I hear the doctor say that Mummy was hit by a car as she crossed the road and that the driver sped off.

My legs go wobbly, all of a sudden, and I feel myself falling. Auntie Comfort grabs me before I hit the ground and guides me to a chair near Mummy's bed.

As I sit with my head back, the young-looking doctor asks, "How are you feeling, dear?"

"Okay," I say, though I still feel funny.

Auntie Comfort smiles gently at me before saying, "This is Maggie's daughter, Esi."

"Oh, right. Well, Esi, it's the shock that's making you feel faint. Keep sitting with your head back. You should feel better soon."

So, I stay leaning back in the chair. From my seat, I see Mummy's bloodied, swollen face clearly. The rest of her body is covered but one of her legs is visible and strapped. She looks in a bad way.

"Please God, I need her." Quietly, I repeat this prayer over and over again, knowing at that moment that whatever her faults, I can't do without Mummy.

Then, I hear the doctor asking Auntie Comfort where my father is.

Auntie Comfort glances at me before saying, "Maggie is a single parent."

"I'll have to contact social services then, as Esi is a minor on her own whilst Maggie is in hospital."

"But I'm her next of kin. She'll stay with me until Maggie is well enough," Auntie Comfort says adamantly.

"I'll have to let social services know anyway. That's the procedure, I'm afraid." The doctor has a firm expression on his face as he smiles at us before going to speak to the nurse tending to Mummy.

I wonder why the doctor is telling social services about me? I've heard of social services, but I don't know what they do or why the doctor needs to tell them about me. It hadn't even occurred to me to think about where I'd be staying now that Mummy was in hospital. Auntie Comfort saying I can stay with her is a relief, although I wonder why she keeps saying she is our next of kin when she is not related to Mummy or me.

My eyes well up. How I wish Nana, Ama, and Auntie Cissy were here now.

18

Bad to worse! That's how life is going.

An Asian looking social worker has just left.

In a long colourful coat lugging a heavy bag full of folders, she turned up at Auntie Comfort's flat this morning and scrutinised everything before asking to see Mummy's flat too. After that, she dropped the bombshell that I may have to move in with a foster family while Mummy's in hospital.

"This is what we normally do with children in your situation," she said, patting the black scarf covering her hair.

"But I'm happy to look after Esi until Maggie is well enough," Auntie Comfort exclaimed. "*I* am her next of kin."

"Yes, I appreciate that," the social worker replied, sounding like she didn't want to argue. "I'll have to speak to my manager about this. I'll be in contact soon."

With that, she left.

I don't know anything about foster carers, but I definitely know I don't want to go and live with one. I want to stay right here with Auntie Comfort, Kojo, and Uncle Kofi until Mummy is back home. Isn't it bad enough that I'm worried about how well Mummy will recover? Now I have to worry about this too.

Yesterday, when Auntie Comfort and I returned to the hospital in the morning to see Mummy, the doctor told us that Mummy was being kept sedated because there's a swelling around her brain. He said that he couldn't tell how long it will take for the swelling to go down, but that it's only when the swelling subsides that Mummy can be taken off sedation and an assessment made of any damage to her brain.

I'm still struggling with this news. What if Mummy has got a brain injury? What will happen then?

Auntie Comfort has assured me many times since the social worker left that I won't be moving anywhere. But I can't help but wonder what she will do if Social Services come to get me. Can she stop them?

The gloominess of the skies I see through the living room window match my mood. I'm sitting with Kojo who is trying to cheer me up by getting me to listen to music with him. Uncle Kofi has gone out especially to buy my favourite Buns bread from an African shop in Hayes. But still, I cannot stop thinking about my predicament. If only I'd never left Ghana. If only Mummy had come to live there instead. Then none of this would be happening.

The phone suddenly rings twice, then goes quiet.

A couple of minutes later, Auntie Comfort walks into the living room saying, "Esi, your Grandma is on the phone."

I was inconsolable yesterday when I spoke to Nana, after Auntie Comfort had called to tell her that Mummy had been hospitalised the night before.

"I am so sorry, Esi," Nana said over and over again. "I wish I could be there with you."

"Please come," I pleaded in the end.

"It is not that straightforward, Esi," Nana explained, sounding guilt-ridden. "I have to get a British visa first."

Thinking about it now, I feel bad because I know Nana will be really worried about me and I don't want to add to her worries, so I put on my brave voice and say, "Hello, Nana."

"Hello, my dear Esi," she replies, her voice sounding shaky. Not as much as yesterday. But still shaky. "How are you?"

"I'm okay, Nana."

"I have been praying for you and Maggie. God is good."

"All the time."

"I thank him that Comfort has opened her home to you. At least I know you are in safe hands."

Deciding in that instant not to tell her about the social worker and what she said, I remain silent. I don't want to lie, but I can't tell her something that will make her worry even more.

"I have been to the British High Commission today, Esi," Nana continues. "Cissy is going to help me complete the visa form and take it back. Then we will see what happens."

Though Nana is trying to sound upbeat, somehow I sense that she doesn't believe that she'll get a visa.

Auntie Cissy comes on after Nana. She and Ama were at school when Auntie Comfort called yesterday. "*Kafra*, Esi. I am so sorry," Auntie Cissy says, then starts crying as Nana says in the background, "*Gyae su*. Stop crying, Cissy. You are not helping her." Ama comes on too, trying to be brave for me.

When the call ends, one thought is going round and round in my head. *I am on my own in London.*

I feel faint and shaky. My chest feels tight. How am I going to manage?

Kojo, Auntie Comfort, and Uncle Kofi are trying their best to help, but for how long will they do that? After all, I'm not their family. What will happen then? Will I end up in foster care?

As tears well up in my eyes, I say to Auntie Comfort and Kojo, "I think I will go and lie down for a bit."

"Are you okay?" Auntie Comfort asks looking concerned as Kojo gazes at me with sympathy.

"Yes, I'm alright," I say, even though that is far from the truth. I hastily retreat to the guest room and shut the door. I flop on the bed and let the tears I've been holding back fall onto the pillow. I know I shouldn't feel sorry for myself because Mummy is the one in hospital, but I do feel very sorry for myself. What will become of me?

There is a knock before the door swings open and Auntie Comfort walks in. I sit up, wiping my face with the back of my hand.

"Kofi is back with the Buns bread," she says gently before coming to perch next to me on the bed. "Esi, don't hide away and cry. Kofi, Kojo, and I all want to help. This is a difficult time. Don't think you have to bear it on your own. Come and talk to me."

"Why are you helping me, Auntie Comfort?" I blurt out.

She looks at me with kind eyes and smiles. "How can I not help Esi? If Kojo was in a similar situation, I would hope that someone would help him too. Not to mention that I'm very fond of you and Maggie.

"How come you are our next of kin when you are not related to us?" It's something that has puzzled me.

"A few weeks before you arrived, your mother asked me to be next of kin for you and her and I was happy to help. I was touched that she trusted me enough to ask."

79

"You must be good friends with her then?"

Auntie Comfort nods. "I met her at Anointed International about three years ago. She really had her guard up when she first started coming to church. She had this funny habit of leaving just before the service ended as if to avoid having to talk to people. But then one Sunday, I was on door duty at church and when she got up to leave, I talked her into staying and having a cup of tea with me and Kofi after church. Since then, I looked out for her at church and she gradually let her guard down a little with me. When she told me she was bringing her daughter over and was looking for somewhere to live, I told her that the tenant in our buy-to-let flat was about to move out. She came to see the flat and took it. Then—"

The doorbell rings.

19

"Good morning, Sister Comfort."

Pastor Timothy walks into Auntie Comfort's hall confidently. He looks bigger and older than I remember, but then I haven't seen him since that first Sunday at Anointed International.

Walking in behind him is Ms Mary in a very elaborate blue dress. There was a time when I would've been so happy to see her without Mummy, hoping to get her to talk about my father. But now, the very idea makes me feel like I'm betraying Mummy and I don't want to do that in case it weakens my prayer to God for her full recovery.

At breakfast before the social worker came, Auntie Comfort mentioned that Pastor Timothy would be coming to see us today, but she didn't mention Ms Mary and, judging from the way she's just said, "Oh, hello Sister Mary. This is a surprise," I don't think she knew Ms Mary was coming.

"Good morning, Sister Comfort," Ms Mary replies with a big smile as she looks around inquisitively. "When Pastor told me about what had happened to Esi's mother and that he was coming to visit her, I said I would accompany him. After all, Esi is a member of the Youth Fellowship and I know her father's family."

"I see," says Auntie Comfort with a slight frown.

"My dear," Pastor Timothy exclaims loudly as he spots me standing near the guest room door. I move forward and as I near him, he reaches for my hand and shakes it. "We were all so sad to hear the news about your mother," he says. "Ms Mary and I are here to pray with you and Sister Comfort, Brother Kofi, and young Kojo at this difficult time."

"Please come through," Auntie Comfort says, leading the way to the living room.

As we walk in, Uncle Kofi and Kojo get up from the sofa to greet Pastor Timothy and Ms Mary. Then Auntie Comfort asks us all to sit and Uncle Kofi offers to make tea.

"Esi, all the Youth Fellowship teachers wanted me to tell you that we are praying for you and your mother," Ms Mary says, looking at me.

"Thank you," I say, though it crosses my mind that the Youth Fellowship teachers may not even remember me since I've only been to the church once.

Auntie Comfort starts to tell the Pastor and Ms Mary what has happened, including the social worker coming to see us today.

"But Esi has a family," interrupts Ms Mary, "so why should social services be getting involved?"

"With Maggie hospitalised, there is no adult family member in London to look after her," responds Auntie Comfort. "That's why she's living with me. Luckily, Maggie had already made me her next of kin."

Ms Mary frowns. "But Esi's —"

"Sorry, I took so long," says Uncle Kofi, cutting off Ms Mary, as he emerges from the kitchen clutching a tray laden with piping hot mugs and a plate with slices of cake. Everyone apart from me tucks into the cake as they drink their hot tea. I don't eat or drink. I don't think my tummy could hold anything down right now.

Once they've finished, Pastor Timothy says, "Let's stand and join hands in prayer." Kojo and Uncle Kofi get up from the dining table where they've been sitting and come to stand beside me as does Auntie Comfort. As we join hands in a circle, the pastor continues, "Friends, there is great power in prayer. In Psalm 107, the Bible says, 'Then they cried to the LORD in their trouble, and he delivered them from their distress. He made the storm be still, and the waves of the sea were hushed.' So let's submit Esi and Maggie to God in prayer."

Pastor Timothy's prayer is comforting and touching at the beginning, but as the prayer gets increasingly loud and he keeps using lots of words when one will do, the prayer feels less so. It's a relief when he finally finishes.

Pastor Timothy and Ms Mary get ready to leave. As Uncle Kofi walks them out, Ms Mary says to me, "Stay strong Esi. God is with you." She pauses and looks like she is about to say something else, but then walks off as Auntie Comfort approaches.

What was that about?

20

It is Wednesday. Still no word from the social worker. I'm back at school for the third day since Mummy was hospitalised. Being back has not been easy. I feel I have to put on a brave face and carry on as normal when things don't feel normal at all.

On Sunday, Auntie Comfort told me that I needed to go back to school. We had gone to see Mummy in the morning instead of going to church with Kojo and Uncle Kofi. I said I didn't want to go to church as I couldn't face having to deal with lots of questions about Mummy, and Auntie Comfort seemed to understand.

But when I got to Mummy, all I did was sit and cry in the chair beside her hospital bed. Auntie Comfort consoled me, but then suggested that it may not be a good idea for me to come to the hospital every day. She would visit every day and I could come with her every two to three days. Once Mummy got off sedation, then I could visit every day again. At first, I vehemently refused. Auntie Comfort said I had to keep busy so I wasn't always thinking and worrying about Mummy. She added that Mummy wouldn't be happy about me missing school. That, I knew, was definitely true. So I agreed, that from Monday, I would go back to school.

It is lunchtime and having just thrown away my lunch rubbish in the bins in the covered outdoor sitting area, I'm about to head back to where Kojo, Mohammed, and Karen are sitting on the playing fields.

"Essi."

I turn around to see Lisa, Imogen, Chloe, and Denise right behind me.

"Hi," I say tentatively. What now? Despite Lisa taking every opportunity to have a dig at me, I've managed to avoid any big confrontation with her. But I may not be so lucky today and I'm really not in the mood to deal with her and her cronies.

"We not good enough for you anymore?" Lisa asks moving up close, as Imogen, Chloe and Denise gather in beside her.

"I don't know what you mean," I say.

"You don't know what I mean? You know exactly what I mean. Why have you dissed us for those three numpties?" she says, pointing in the direction of Kojo, Karen, and Mohammed.

Though I don't know what numpty means, I guess it's an insult. Lisa is clearly spoiling for a fight. I've seen her get into fights with other children for the flimsiest of reasons. I don't want any *wahala* from her.

"I am not dissing you," I say. "Kojo and I have become friends because we live next to each other."

I don't mention anything about me living with Kojo at the moment. Lisa and her chums are the last people I want to know. The only people who know at school, apart from Mr Herbert and Mrs Pier, are Mohammed and Karen as well as Kojo, of course. I told them all that I did not want anyone else at school to be told.

"Don't give me any of that crap," says Lisa. "I know when I'm being given the cold shoulder."

What is this girl saying now?

85

"Don't you understand what I'm saying, Essi?" Lisa's eyes narrow as her expression turns mean. "Is your English not up to scratch?"

"Of course it's not," says Imogen. "She just came from Africa, innit."

Denise jumps in. "Yeah, haven't you heard how strong her African accent is?"

They start to snigger. Anger courses through my body. With all that is going on with Mummy, the last thing I need is this rubbish.

Lisa leans forward and touches my hair deliberately. I move my head away as she says, "Your hair is so interesting, Essi."

"It's called an afro, innit?" pipes up Chloe. "Very seventies."

"You really should do something about it. You look like a boy." Denise sneers at me, her eyes flicking toward her friends to make sure they laugh.

"Yes, a boy in a skirt," Lisa adds, laughing.

The rest of them laugh too.

I know they are trying to goad me and that I shouldn't rise to their bait. But I'm so angry. Who do they think they are? What gives them the right to make fun of me, as if they are better than me?

"Please leave me alone," I say through gritted teeth.

"Please leave me alone," they all mimic in unison, followed by peals of laughter.

My anger erupts. I start screaming as tears of anger pour down my face. "Go away and leave me alone. You have no right to talk to me like that."

"What's going on?"

Kojo is standing next to me, with Mohammed and Karen beside him. I didn't see them come up. Behind them, other children are standing and staring in my direction. I'm so embarrassed.

"Don't ask *me* what's going on," says Lisa. "Ask your mate. I think she's losing it."

Kojo moves to stand right in front of Lisa. "Bog off, Lisa. I don't want to see you bothering Esi again."

"Oh, it's like that, is it?" Lisa says smirking. "You and Esi have got the hots for each other."

"Get lost, Lisa," Kojo says.

"C'mon, girls. Let's go and leave these losers," Lisa says, before walking off with her cronies in tow.

Kojo, Karen, and Mohammed gather around me. Mohammed asks, "You okay, Esi?"

"Yes, I'm alright," I say. I'm still embarrassed, but the tears have dried up. Kojo getting rid of Lisa has made me feel a little better.

Karen says, "You should speak to Mr Herbert about getting a different buddy and sitting away from Lisa. She's known for holding a grudge and she'll make your life hell if she remains your buddy. I bet you can do without that. We'll come with you to speak to him if you'd like."

I nod and with the three of them next to me, we walk into school.

21

"It's still chucking it down," says Kojo, as we stand under the covered area watching other children making a mad dash through the rain. I assume chucking it down means pouring with rain. Even now, I have to pause and think about these UK phrases that I'd never heard of before in Ghana.

School has ended and Kojo and I should be walking home. Mohammed and Karen have already left but we've been waiting to see if the rain will ease. So far, there is no sign of that happening.

"I think we'll have to brave it, Esi," Kojo says.

I nod in agreement.

We zip up our coats, put our hoods on and step out.

We walk as fast as we can but soon we are wet and soggy.

When we finally reach the small parade of shops around the corner from the flats, I'm relieved that we don't have much further to go. As we walk swiftly past the shops, I think I hear, "Esi. Kojo."

"Did you hear that?" I say to Kojo, slowing down.

"Hear what?" says Kojo grumpily, not happy about me not keeping up.

"Somebody is calling us. Listen."

"Esi. Kojo."

We look back and, leaning out of a window above Kumar's Emporium, is an Asian boy waving excitedly at us. It's Savaan.

Savaan became my new class buddy today. Yes, he is geeky and talks way too much, but sitting next to him is so much better than sitting next to Lisa. Lisa now sits next to Hugh. Hugh's nickname is 'Bone crusher' because we are all a little afraid of him. I would love to see Lisa dare to annoy him. He'll put her in her place for sure and it'll serve her right.

Mr Herbert spoke to Lisa and her mates after our confrontation yesterday and it seems to have done the trick because they've steered well clear of me all day and that has been a real relief. Not having to deal with Lisa is one less thing to worry about with all that is going on in my life.

Despite the rain, I smile and wave at Savaan. "What are you doing up there?"

"This is where I live," he yells back. "My parents own the shop below."

"I have walked past this shop so many times," I say. "I've never seen you before."

"Oh, I've seen him in there before," says Kojo, pulling his hood lower against the rain.

"Where do you two live?" asks Savaan.

"Round the corner on Carlton Road. Kojo is my neighbour," I reply, not mentioning that I'm living with Kojo now.

"You're really close. Hopefully, I'll see you around," says Savaan.

"That would be good." I blink as rain falls in my eyes. "We'd better go. We're getting soaked."

"Oh yes, of course, sorry," says Savaan. "See you tomorrow."

We wave goodbye and continue walking. At the end of the road, we turn right onto our road and continue walking briskly.

"Look," says Kojo, a couple of minutes later. "I think there's a man outside your Mum's front door."

I look and, though it is raining and we are still quite far away, there is definitely a man outside Mummy's door. We keep walking and as we get a bit closer, I can make out that the man is black, tallish with short cropped hair, and wearing a brownish leather jacket. We see him put what looks like a note through Mummy's letterbox.

As he turns to walk away, my heart starts beating fast as I catch sight of his face. Even from afar, there's something about him that looks like the man in the photo in my rucksack. Could that be my father? I start running.

Kojo cries out behind me. "What are you doing, Esi?"

The man walks briskly towards the main road and soon he has turned the corner out of sight. I keep running after him. At the end of the road, I look for him but can't see him anywhere. I turn and run back, brushing past Kojo, who has been running to catch up with me.

"What has got into you, Esi?" he asks.

"I think that man is my father," I shout out, still running.

I run to Mummy's front door and dig out my key from my rucksack. I open the door and see a folded piece of paper on the carpet. Picking it up, I sit on the bottom stair and unfold it.

I see the name at the bottom of the note and start trembling just as Kojo gets to the door. It was my father I'd seen. And I'd missed him. What if he never comes back?

22

I run past a startled Kojo and ring the doorbell at Auntie Comfort's flat.

"Hang on a minute," Kojo calls out as he picks up my rucksack and locks Mummy's front door with my key, which is still in the lock.

"Oh good. You are here," Auntie Comfort says as she opens the front door. "I was getting worried. Come in out of the rain."

As I walk in followed by Kojo carrying his rucksack and mine, Auntie Comfort looks at me and asks, "What's the matter?" as Kojo hands me back my key before dumping the bags in the hall.

"My father has been here," I burst out, still shocked at what has just happened.

"Your father has been here?" repeats Auntie Comfort, looking confused.

"Kojo and I had just turned onto the road when we saw a man outside Mummy's front door. He put a note through the letterbox and started to walk away. I thought he looked a bit like my father so I started running after him, but I lost him on the main road," I say, barely pausing for air.

"So how do you know it was definitely your father?"

Waving the note, I say, "Because I went into Mummy's flat and found a note behind the front door. It's signed Solomon. That is my father's name."

Auntie Comfort takes the note. "Okay. First things first, you must be freezing in your wet things. Take your coats off and change into something warm. Then come and join me in the living room."

Kojo and I do as we are told and go to our rooms to get changed before heading to the living room. I'm shaking, but not from the cold. Father's here. In London. I can't believe it.

As we all sit on the black leather sofa, Auntie Comfort says, "Would you mind if I read the note, Esi?"

"No." I haven't actually read the note. All I saw was Father's name.

Auntie Comfort takes the note from the centre table and starts to read it out loud.

Dear Maggie,

I know you will be shocked to get this note, but I heard about your accident and wanted to see you. How is Esi? I hear she is in London too. There is no one answering your door so maybe you are still in hospital. This is my mobile number in London. Please call me. We need to talk.

Love Solomon

His number is there. Right there, in front of me. "I want to call him," I say.

"Yes Esi, I can understand that you want to," Auntie Comfort says, refolding the note and placing it on the table. "But because I don't know what's gone on between your mother and father, I don't want to open a can of worms when your mother is in hospital."

Auntie Comfort pauses for a while before adding, "I think I'll call your grandmother and explain what has happened to her and see what she thinks. Okay?"

"Okay," I say, reluctantly.

Auntie Comfort gets the phone and dials Nana's number.

"Good afternoon, Auntie Nancy," she begins. "*Brebiara ye.*
Everything is okay. Esi is fine. Maggie is still sedated. Esi and I will
be going to see her this evening, so I'll let you know if there is any
change after that. I'm calling about a different matter. A note has
just been posted through Maggie's front door by Solomon."

She waits, listening. "Yes, it would appear that he's in London. I
didn't see him myself. Esi and Kojo were the ones who saw a man
from afar at Maggie's door. They didn't get to him before he
walked away. But when Esi opened the door, she found the note
from him."

Again, she waits. "I don't know how he could know where she
lives. He left his mobile number in the note and Esi would like to
call him."

This time as she waits for an answer, she looks at me, frowning
slightly. "Alright, hang on. I'll put Esi on the phone."

I take the phone, hoping that Nana isn't going to tell me not to
call Father.

"Good afternoon, Nana."

"Hello, my dear Esi."

I get straight to the point. "Nana, I want to call him."

"Esi, I know. I appreciate that you've been wanting to know your
father for a long time, but I have to ask that you wait for your
mother to recover before you contact him."

"Why Nana? Why can't I just call him now?"

"Esi, with the way things are between your mother and father, I don't want events to unfold and for you to have no-one there to support you. Cissy and I are not there. Comfort is looking after you, but I cannot allow her to get dragged into your mother and father's issues. It would not be fair. Esi, *mepa wo kyɛw*, please, be patient. Keep the number safe so you can use it when the time comes."

"Alright, Nana," I say, even though everything in me wants to go ahead and call my father. I hand the phone back to Auntie Comfort and sit down glumly next to Kojo.

Kojo nudges me and says, "Alright?"

"I'm disappointed, but I'm alright."

"But look on the bright side," he says. "You now know that your father is in London. Did you know that before?"

"No. I had no idea where he was."

"And you have his mobile number so you know how to reach him. Did you know that before?"

"No, I didn't."

"Kojo is right." Auntie Comfort says as she puts the phone down. "You do have things to be cheerful about. Now, both of you, go and get your homework done. I'll make dinner so we can eat before Kofi gets back from work. When he gets home, Esi, you and I will go to the hospital to see your mother. Okay?"

"Yes," I say, feeling a little mollified.

23

Thursday evening. Auntie Comfort and I are walking to ICU. Again.

I hope there is good news this time.

Good things have happened in the last couple of weeks. The first was Father's surprise appearance last week Thursday. The second was that yesterday the social worker finally called Auntie Comfort and Social services are allowing me to stay with her. Thank God! Until Mummy is back home, the social worker will check on me from time to time like she did this afternoon after school, but I don't care. All I wanted was not to be forced to go and live with complete strangers.

Auntie Comfort rings the buzzer for the ICU ward. After speaking to a nurse through the intercom, the door is unlocked and we walk in, heading to Mummy's cubicle.

I'm sure that there is a saying that things happen in threes. So maybe the third good thing that will happen will be positive news about Mummy. So far, there has been little change in the two weeks that she has been in hospital. There is still a swelling around her brain and she remains sedated. Fear that she will be brain damaged never leaves me. It is always there at the back of my mind. I've been waking in the middle of the night, unable to go back to sleep as I worry about her. Not knowing is hard to deal with. I cannot bear to think about what life will be like if she is brain damaged. Yes, before the accident, I was finding Mummy difficult, but I'd rather have her back the way she was than brain damaged.

Auntie Comfort and I walk into Mummy's cubicle.

"Good morning," a nurse tending to Mummy greets us with a smile.

"Good morning," Auntie Comfort and I reply. We've met this nurse a few times.

"Is your father coming today?" the nurse asks, looking at me.

"Father?" Auntie Comfort splutters as I stand speechless.

"The young lady's father. Maggie's husband," the nurse replies, looking puzzled.

"Why would my father be coming today?" I ask.

"He was here yesterday."

"He was?" I repeat, shocked.

"Yes, he said he'd not come sooner because he had been out of the country. Did you not know?" The nurse looks from Auntie Comfort's face to mine in obvious confusion.

I shake my head to say no as my mind works overtime. What was Father doing here? How did he know that Mummy was in ICU? There are many hospitals in London so how did he know to come to this particular one? His note said he'd heard about her accident, but who had told him?

"Maggie and her husband are not together anymore," Auntie Comfort explains to the nurse.

"Oh sorry, I didn't know," the nurse says apologetically. "We wouldn't have let him in if we'd known that Maggie wouldn't want it."

"It's fine," says Auntie Comfort. "I don't know that she wouldn't have wanted it. I don't think she knew that he was in London."

"So what should be done the next time he comes to see her?" the nurse asks.

Auntie Comfort turns and looks at me as she thinks about what to say. As far as I am concerned, it doesn't feel right for Father to be prevented from seeing Mummy. After all, I might be able to meet him here if he comes to visit her.

"Father shouldn't be stopped from seeing Mummy," I say firmly.

Auntie Comfort looks unsure.

"They are still married," I add.

"Oh I see," says Auntie Comfort, looking surprised. "Well, in that case, he should see Maggie."

"Alright, I'll let my colleagues know. The doctor is doing his rounds and should be here any moment now," says the nurse before heading off. Auntie Comfort and I sit next to sleeping Mummy, listening to the beeps and the quiet chatter outside her cubicle whilst we wait for the doctor.

Later, as we drive back to the flat, I mull over what the doctor said. He informed us that Mummy had been scanned yesterday and her swelling had come down slightly. So it was still a waiting game, but things were moving in the right direction.

"Thank God," said Auntie Comfort, looking pleased. I wasn't so pleased. This wasn't the good news I was hoping for. It is taking so long and all the while, I don't know what injury Mummy may have sustained.

Tomorrow is the last day of school before half term begins which means that for a whole week, I won't even have school to distract me. I just know that I'm going to spend the whole half term dwelling on Mummy.

My first half term in London.

In Ghana, I always looked forward to half term. It was a chance to do more of the things I loved—reading, spending time in the bakery with Nana plus hanging out with Ama and my friends in the neighbourhood. Then there were the trips to Labadi Beach with Auntie Cissy. She would treat Ama and me to lunch in a restaurant overlooking the sea before we went for a walk on the sand, gazing at the sea and the people on the beach.

But this half term, apart from going to see Mummy, I've no real idea what I'll be doing. I don't want to ask, either.

Kojo told me that normally he, Uncle Kofi, and Auntie Comfort go away for half term, but they were not doing that this half term. I can't help wondering if this is because of Mummy and me. That makes me feel guilty. But what can I do?

Later, as I'm going to bed, I have a strong urge to dig out the family photo of Mummy, my father, and me from my rucksack and gaze at it. Father turning up twice unexpectedly has left me feeling that I may well meet him, although I don't know when. What will I do then? After all these years of wishing for him, I don't know what I'll do when I actually see him. What if he doesn't like me? What if he didn't come to see me before because he doesn't want me? But his note asks about me, and that makes me feel a little hopeful. I put the photo under my pillow before laying my head down. Oddly, it makes me feel better.

24

Red, yellow, orange, brown, green.

These are the different coloured leaves I've spotted so far.

On the trees and on the ground.

Squashed under our boots as we walk.

Some even match the exact golden yellow of my jumper, brown trousers and boots.

Of course, I prefer the sunshine of Ghana, although it does sometimes get too hot. But actually, "Autumn is beautiful," I think out loud. "Look at all the colours, Kojo."

Kojo shrugs, as he looks around. "Suppose so."

His lack of enthusiasm makes me smile. Today, unlike most of the half term, he is wearing something other than his tracksuits. His black combat boots and matching leather jacket over his grey jumper and blue jeans look smart.

I poke his arm and say, "I'm glad you decided to come to Savaan's lunch." I wasn't sure he would come until this morning.

With another shrug, he says, "It's something to do, I guess."

"Well, I'm looking forward to it," I say.

We bumped into Savaan at his parents' shop on Monday. Uncle Kofi was home that day and was looking forward to a leisurely breakfast of sweet Buns bread and Milo, but there was no Milo in the flat, so he sent Kojo and me to Kumar's Emporium to buy Milo. Savaan must have seen us entering the shop because he came rushing to say hello. He helped us find the Milo and then asked if Kojo and I would be interested in coming to join him and his family for his birthday lunch on Thursday. Surprised, I immediately said yes, even though Kojo didn't look very enthusiastic and I'd not asked Auntie Comfort or Uncle Kofi if I could go. I like Savaan. He is really sweet and since coming from Ghana, apart from Kojo, I've not visited anyone in their home and I've missed doing that. Visiting friends had been such a regular part of my life in Ghana.

Luckily, Auntie Comfort and Uncle Kofi were happy for us to go when I asked them back at the flat.

So today, Kojo and I are walking towards Savaan's place with his wrapped present and card clutched in my hand.

I continue to gaze at the colour all around us as we walk. How is it that I'm only really noticing the colours of autumn today?

Maybe it's because this is the happiest I've felt for a long time.

Kojo looks at me. "You look like the cat that's got the cream, Esi."

"Is that another of your UK sayings? What does it mean?"

Kojo chuckles. "It means you look happy with yourself."

"Of course, I'm happy Kojo. I'm on cloud nine. Mummy is awake! Thank you, God," I say loudly, my arms up in the air.

Kojo smiles at me.

How I have been thanking God since Tuesday. That morning, Auntie Comfort noticed a voice message had been left on her phone by the hospital. The voice message from the night before said that Mummy was being taken off sedation because her scan on Monday showed that her swelling had suddenly gone down drastically. Auntie Comfort called the hospital straight away and it was confirmed that Mummy was no longer sedated. She and I got in the car immediately, leaving Kojo in the flat, to drive to the hospital, even though we'd originally planned to visit Mummy in the evening. On the way to the hospital, I couldn't stop thinking about what the doctor had said about not being able to tell the damage to Mummy's brain until she was off sedation.

Please God, I prayed, *I've kept my promise to stop complaining about Mummy. Please let her be okay.*

Once Auntie Comfort parked her car in the hospital car park, we rushed up to ICU. In Mummy's cubicle, we found the doctor and a nurse standing next to Mummy's bed. The doctor smiled as we walked in and stepped back from the bed, revealing Mummy still lying with her right leg in a cast, but with her eyes open.

"Mummy!" I shouted, relief coursing through my veins.

"Esi," she replied with a croaky voice and a broad smile.

I ran to her and flung myself on her chest, saying, "Thank you, God. Thank you, God."

When I finally lifted my face, Mummy was looking at me with a teary smile. She looked weak but her eyes were alert. Her cheeks looked less chubby and I could see her cheekbones. She'd lost some weight! Strange that I was only noticing it now when I'd seen her so often in hospital.

"I'm so happy you're awake, Mummy." I clutched her hand, my need to hold onto her overwhelming.

"I'm so glad to be awake to see you, Esi." Mummy squeezed my hand. "I'm sorry you have had to go through this. How have you been?"

"Esi has been such a trouper," said Auntie Comfort, coming round the other side of the bed.

"Oh, Comfort, *medaase*." Mummy stretched out her other hand to her. "Thank you for looking after Esi. You've been such a good friend."

Auntie Comfort held Mummy's hand and gave her a hug. "It was my pleasure, Maggie. We've loved having Esi staying with us. I'm just very relieved to see you awake."

We chatted for a while before Mummy began to look exhausted. The doctor asked us to let her rest so we kissed Mummy goodbye and said we would be back the next day. The doctor took Auntie Comfort and I to one side and told us that Mummy's leg will remain in a cast for quite a while before it completely healed but that he was cautiously optimistic that there was no long-term injury to Mummy's brain. He would keep Mummy under observation until he was satisfied that it was safe for her to go home.

When Auntie Comfort called Nana to tell her the news after we got back to the flat, Nana's shouts of joy were so loud I could hear them even though I wasn't on the phone. When I got on the phone, Nana kept repeating that God was answering her prayers and that we serve a mighty God. It was then that she admitted that she hadn't been given a British visa, so she couldn't come. I was disappointed, but since I'd suspected for a while that she wouldn't be able to come, I wasn't surprised. Moreover, with Mummy now awake, I didn't need Nana to be here as before.

Yesterday, at the hospital, Auntie Comfort called Nana on her mobile so Mummy could speak to her. As they spoke, Mummy got very emotional and started to cry. That set me off too, crying tears of relief.

We've not as yet told Mummy about Father.

Nana didn't think it was a good idea to tell her straight away. She feared that the shock might setback Mummy's recovery, so she told Auntie Comfort and me to wait for Mummy to get stronger before we told her. Anyway, there has been no sign of Father since his visit to the hospital. What that means, I don't know, and I am trying not to dwell on it.

This morning, the doctor gave us the amazing news that all being well, Mummy could come home as early as Saturday. I was so happy when he told us that I couldn't stop myself from jumping up and down.

Tomorrow, Auntie Comfort, Uncle Kofi, Kojo and I will go and visit Mummy in hospital, and then we're going to get Mummy's flat ready for her return. The flat hasn't been cleaned since Mummy had the accident. I've only gone in for my clothes but being there without her has felt too strange to stay for any length of time.

So yes, I'm in a very good mood and really looking forward to Savaan's lunch. I'm sure it's a relief to Kojo that I'm not moody and dwelling on my problems as before. I probably haven't been a great friend for the last few weeks. I feel bad about that.

I glance at him.

He hasn't said anything, but I think he hasn't had the best half term. With Auntie Comfort going back and forth to hospital with me and Uncle Kofi being at work for a large part of the week, he has spent quite a lot of time on his own in the flat, which cannot have been that much fun.

Having said that, there have been some fun moments.

On Monday, Uncle Kofi took us out. After Auntie Comfort and I got back from the hospital in the afternoon, we all went to the cinema in Uxbridge to watch *Nutty Professor II* where Uncle Kofi treated us to popcorn and drinks as well. But, as I sat watching the movie, I started feeling guilty about having fun when Mummy was lying in a hospital bed. That spoilt my enjoyment but I didn't say anything to the others. After the movie, we went shopping in Uxbridge town centre. It was my first time ever there so it should have been exciting, but as we browsed through shops, many of which I'd seen advertised on TV, I continued to feel guilty. In one large shop, with about four floors, Kojo and I chose a birthday card and birthday present - a blue denim jacket - for Savaan which Auntie Comfort paid for. On the way back to the flat, seeing how much Kojo had enjoyed going out with his Dad and Mum, I was glad that I hadn't said anything about my guilt which could have spoilt his fun.

Then, on Wednesday afternoon, still feeling overjoyed at Mummy's progress, I ventured out into the garden with Kojo when the weather wasn't so cold and wet. We had a really good time, swinging on the swings and jumping on the trampoline.

"You're lucky," I said to Kojo, as we came off the trampoline.

"Why do you say that?" he asked looking puzzled.

"You have all of this to play with. I've never had play stuff in a garden. Mummy's flat hasn't got a garden and there were no playthings in Nana's garden — just plants."

"You can always come and play here if you want," was Kojo's response. But now looking back, I wonder if I came across as envious to him. That makes me feel a bit rotten. But, we've reached Kumar's Emporium, so I push my thoughts to the back of my mind.

"Should we go in and ask if we can go up?" I ask Kojo, as we peer inside the shop. It is busy with customers and Savaan's father is behind the counter.

"No. Remember Savaan told us to ring the bell by the black side door and he would let us in."

"Oh yeah, you're right."

We walk to the door by the side of the shop and Kojo rings the doorbell.

The door flings open and there stands Savaan in jeans and a check shirt with a wide grin on his face.

"Hi guys," he says, stepping back to let us in.

We walk into a narrow corridor with busy wallpaper and then up some stairs to the entrance of Savaan's family flat above the shop. Standing at the entrance is Savaan's Mum, her dark hair just visible under the light cloth draped over her head and shoulders. She is wearing a light blue long top and matching trousers.

"Come in. You are very welcome," she says with a warm smile. We walk into the flat and are ushered into the living room where Savaan's two brothers are sitting sprawled on the sofa. They look up and say, "Hi," as Kojo and I walk in. Savaan's Mum says, "Rafi, Anik, move up and make space for Savaan's guests."

His brothers vacate the sofa to sit on two brown leather chairs by the window and Kojo and I sit on the sofa. Savaan comes to sit beside me. I hand him his present and card. He opens it straight away and exclaims, "Wow. Thanks, guys."

"Glad you like it," I say.

"I love it," he replies. "Well, I hope you're hungry because Mum has cooked lots of food."

"You can say that again," says Rafi, who is a year younger than Savaan. Anik, the eldest brother, nods and laughs.

Savaan leads us to the dining room which opens onto the kitchen. The flat is larger than it looks from outside.

Savaan and his brothers weren't exaggerating about the food. On a long wooden table, there are four different kinds of curry. Savaan's mother tells Kojo and I the name of each curry, but the names don't register. There is also red-looking chicken, coloured rice, flat puffy bread, and vegetable pastry parcels on the table. I put a bit of everything on the plate that I'm handed by Savaan's mother. With my heaped plate, I sit down on one of the wooden dining chairs and start to eat. I'm not familiar with Bangladeshi food, but what I am eating is delicious. I eat everything on my plate. The curry with spinach and chicken is the best. I am stuffed, but I think I could eat a little bit more of that.

"Esi, you have big appetite. I like a girl who likes to eat," Savaan's mother says.

I look up to see her looking at me with a smile. I'm mortified, especially when the others start laughing. She must think I'm a pig. I decide against getting any more food.

We go back to the living room once everyone has finished eating. Savaan gets out a Monopoly box from the large wood and glass cabinet in the living room.

"Do you want to play?" he asks.

"Sure," I say, as Kojo nods his head.

Savaan lays out the Monopoly board on the wooden centre table. We kneel around the table, as do his brothers, and start to play. This is the first board game I've played since coming to London. I'd forgotten how much I enjoyed playing board games. Ama and I used to play them all the time, often on the large teak table in Nana's dining room. Ludo was our favourite. Nana and Auntie Cissy would sometimes join in but Nana would always get the rules mixed up and Auntie Cissy would get so competitive. Ama, not wanting to be outdone by her mother, would try to win by whatever means.

"Esi, it's your turn. What are you waiting for?" I snap out of my daydream to see Kojo staring at me with a slight frown as are Savaan and his brothers.

"Sorry," I say. A little flustered, I quickly play my turn.

In next to no time, everyone is in high spirits and engrossed in the game. It's only when Savaan's mother comes in with his birthday cake that I realise how dark it's become. Kojo looks at his watch and says to me, "We'd better get going before my Mum and Dad get worried."

After Savaan blows out his candles and cuts the cake, I tell him that Kojo and I have to go. His mother cuts some birthday cake for us to take away. Holding the cake wrapped in cling film, we say goodbye to Savaan's Mum and brothers before heading down with Savaan.

Soon, we are waving goodbye and setting off back to the flat in the cold.

"That was cool," Kojo says with a sideways glance at me as we walk briskly.

I smile. "Yeah, I really enjoyed it too." Liking Savaan even more now that I've spent time with him and his family, I've got the same contented feeling that I often had when Ama and I had been to visit a friend. Maybe if I do more of the things I enjoyed in Ghana here in London, it might feel more like home.

"Oh!" That sudden thought startles me.

"Are you okay?" Kojo asks.

"Yeah, I'm fine," I reply with a nod, and at that moment, I feel more positive than ever about my life in London.

25

Mummy is home, lying on the living room sofa, talking to Nana on the phone.

In the kitchen, Auntie Comfort is putting away the food she's cooked.

I'm in Mummy's bedroom singing to myself as I get Mummy's bed ready.

Auntie Comfort and I went to get Mummy from hospital this morning. When we got back to the flat, it was a struggle for Mummy to climb the stairs. With her leg in plaster, she had to hobble up slowly with her crutches. By the time she got upstairs, she was exhausted. Mummy will need a lot of help over the next few weeks so I'll have to do a lot more in the flat. But I don't mind. She is home with no brain injury! So I'm happy to do whatever has to be done without any complaint.

"Auntie Nancy has told me to tell Maggie about your father's appearance."

I look up to see Auntie Comfort. She has just walked into Mummy's bedroom.

"Oh," is all I can manage to say, suddenly feeling anxious.

"I'll tell her today before I go. You okay with that?"

"I suppose so," I reply, still feeling worried.

"Esi," Mummy calls out from the living room, "Ama wants to talk to you."

I run to get the handset from Mummy. "Hi," I say to Ama, as I step out to speak to her in my room.

"Hello Cuz," says Ama. "Eh, you must be so relieved that Auntie Maggie is home."

"Relieved is not the word, Ama. I'm ecstatic."

"I had no doubt that she would get better."

"Really?"

"The way we've been praying here, how could she not get better? We've been praying for her at home. All the regulars who come to the bakery have been told to pray for her. The whole Tesano Methodist congregation has been praying for her, as has Nana's women's fellowship group, and Mummy's singing band."

"I didn't know that," I say. I knew Nana, Ama and Auntie Cissy would be praying, but all those people supporting Mummy and me – that's amazing.

"I'm telling you. We have been generating prayer power here."

"Well, it's been powerful prayer power," I say with a smile, "because the doctor is now saying that Mummy should make a full recovery."

"We thank God!"

"I really wish you were here."

"So do I, Esi. I've felt so bad that you've been on your own through all of this."

"At first, I did feel like I was on my own, Ama, but Auntie Comfort, Kojo, and Uncle Kofi have been really good to me. They made me feel like I had family around me."

111

"*Chale*, it is strange to hear you talk this way about people I've never met."

"Maybe you'll get to meet them when you come to visit me one day."

"I really hope so."

After I bid Ama goodbye a few minutes later, I remember that I've never told her that only a few weeks ago, I was thinking of returning to Ghana. But now that God has answered my prayers about Mummy, I feel guilty even thinking about it.

I head back to the living room with the phone. Auntie Comfort is helping Mummy to get up from the sofa. Quickly putting the phone in its stand, I go to help. Auntie Comfort and I walk with Mummy to her bedroom and to her bed. As Mummy lies down with her plastered leg resting on a pile of pillows, Auntie Comfort plumps up the white pillows beneath her head.

Mummy looks content and reaches for my hand. She has been very touchy-feely with me since waking from her sedation, and although I do like this new affectionate Mummy, it's taking some getting used to.

"Maggie," Auntie Comfort starts tentatively, "Esi and I have something to tell you."

"What is it, Comfort?" Mummy asks with a frown.

"When you were in hospital, Esi's father showed up."

"Solomon was here?" Mummy says, clearly shocked. She tries to sit up but struggles. Auntie Comfort leans forward and helps her.

"Yes, he came here and also went to the hospital to see you," I say.

"You met him?" Mummy asks, looking at me, her eyes wide.

"No, I didn't get to meet him," I say, careful to keep my expression blank. "But I saw him standing at the front door when Kojo and I were walking back from school."

"You saw him?" Mummy repeats. "How did you recognise him? The last time you saw him you were four years old."

My face flushes with heat. I guess it's confession time.

"Um, I saw a box of photos under your bed, Mummy."

"Oh." Mummy frowns.

"I had a look inside and found photos of my father. That is how I knew what he looked like," I say quickly, bracing myself for Mummy to tell me off.

But there's no anger. Instead, Mummy asks quietly, "What did Solomon do after you saw him?"

"He didn't see me. Before I could get to him, he had put a note through the door and was walking towards the main road. I ran after him, but by the time I got there, he had disappeared."

"I wonder how he knew my address?" Mummy mutters. "Did you say he left a note?"

"Here," Auntie Comfort says, digging in the side pocket of her black leather bag to get the note out.

Mummy takes the note from Auntie Comfort, but stares at it in her hands, apparently in no rush to open it. She opens the drawer in her white bedside table and puts the note in there. "I think I'll read it later," says Mummy. She turns to me and asks, "Did you see him at the hospital?"

113

"No, one of the nurses who looked after you told Auntie Comfort and me that he had come to see you."

Mummy looks mystified. "Have you seen him since?"

"No, we've not seen him here and it has been about a week since the nurse said she saw him at the hospital," I say.

"Right," says Mummy, looking pensive. "I think I'll rest a little now."

"Let's leave you in peace then," Auntie Comfort says, gesturing for me to walk out of Mummy's room with her.

When Uncle Kofi and Kojo come to greet her later in the afternoon, she is still subdued, as she is when she speaks to Pastor Timothy on the phone after Auntie Comfort calls him. The news about my father has clearly affected her.

That night, after Auntie Comfort, Uncle Kofi, and Kojo return to their flat and Mummy is in her bed asleep, I lie in my bedroom with the lights off. It feels strange to be back here — like I've been away for ages when in truth, it has been about three weeks. I'd gotten so used to Auntie Comfort's guest room but I'm happy to be back with Mummy. Hopefully, Mummy will continue being her new affectionate self and we will get on better than before. And, *please God*, no more nasty surprises.

26

There is someone at the door.

"I'll see who it is," I call out to Mummy, who is lying down in her room. I run down the stairs, wondering who it is. Auntie Comfort, Uncle Kofi, and Kojo passed by to see us before they went to church this morning. It is only eleven, so they can't be back already.

I open the door and find a man standing there.

The same man I saw at the door when Kojo and I were walking back from school.

It's Father.

He looks tall in a long black coat, grey trousers, and a woollen blue pullover. His striking face doesn't look that different from the photos in Mummy's box. It's as if he hasn't aged at all.

I don't know how long I stand and stare. Time just seems to stand still.

He stares, too. "Esi?" he finally says, breaking the silence.

I nod, trying to get to grips with how I'm feeling. I've been longing to meet this man for so long. Yet now that I'm standing in front of him, the feeling that is sweeping over me is not joy, but a wave of deep, burning anger. Why has he not come looking for me in all these years? If he can make the effort now, why has he not done so before?

Father clears his throat. "I am your father," he says hesitantly, as if not sure that I know.

"I know." I finally manage to stop staring and gaze down at my white trainers instead.

"Good," he says. I look back up to see him smiling, looking relieved. That just makes me angrier.

"It is really good to see you Esi. How are you doing?" he asks.

"Okay," I say with a shrug, as I fiddle with the sleeves of my green woolly jumper. Maybe if I speak in monosyllables, my anger won't show for, despite it, I don't want him to go.

"Esi, who is at the door?" Mummy calls out.

I can hear her making her way with her crutches along the landing towards the stairs.

I don't know what to say to her. So I say nothing. I'll let her see for herself who it is. I step back into the hall to give my father space to come in. He takes the cue and walks in, just as Mummy reaches the top of the stairs.

Mummy freezes, shock on her face as she stares down at my father. He stays rooted to the spot in the hall, staring back at her. I shut the front door and stand looking at them.

Finally, Father says, "Hello, Maggie."

"What are you doing here?" Mummy says through gritted teeth.

"I heard about your accident and that you were home from the hospital. I wanted to see how you were."

"Who told you that?"

"Mum's friend, Mary Ofori, goes to your church. She called Mum to tell her and Mum told me."

"Did she tell you where I live as well?"

"Yes, she told Mum and Mum told me."

Mummy shifts on her crutches, as she snaps, "That is really out of order. She shouldn't be handing out my personal information."

"When you were in hospital, she was concerned that Esi was here without a parent. She called to ask why I wasn't coming to take care of her. Mum had to tell her that we were not communicating and no longer together and that I didn't know about the accident." He holds out his hands like he's pleading for her to understand.

Mummy doesn't seem moved. "Great! Mary is such a gossip. She will be spreading my business all over the church. So did you come all the way from Ghana because of this?"

"No, I was about to come to London anyway when I heard. Mum was coming for medical care and I was accompanying her. By the way, she sends her regards."

I stand numb as I try to process everything that I'm hearing. It feels so surreal watching Mummy and Father together after so many years, but it's clear that the animosity between them is still there.

"Well, you can see that Esi and I are okay. You have done your duty, so you can go." She lifts one crutch like she's shooing him away.

"Maggie, please can we just sit down and talk without fighting? It would be good to spend some time with you and Esi."

"Why?" Mummy says in a raised voice, looking irate. "You have not taken any interest in me or Esi in all these years. Why do you want to spend time with us now?"

"You know that is not true, Maggie!" Father responds, sounding angry. "Look, can I please come up? I would really like to talk with you and Esi." He turns to look at me as if seeking my consent. I nod, not knowing what to say. Part of me is happy that he has come because he wanted to talk to me and Mummy. But the other half is still fuming.

I catch Mummy looking at me before she says reluctantly, "Okay, you can come up." Mummy starts to move away on her crutches as Father walks up the stairs with me following him.

Mummy invites Father to sit on the sofa by the wall in the living room. I take Mummy's crutches off her as she lowers herself into the armchair furthest away from the sofa. I lean the crutches against the wall and am about to sit down on the armchair next to her when she says, "Esi, can you please bring some water for your father?"

"Yes, Mummy."

In the kitchen, I can hear Mummy and Father talking in the living room. Not the actual words, but the hum of their voices. Mummy must have wanted me out so that they could speak without me being there. I slowly go through the motions of getting a tray out of the tall kitchen cupboard, taking out three glasses from the wall cupboard by the sink and putting them on the tray along with a jug of water out of the fridge.

Mummy and Father's voices sound angry. I'm not sure that I want to go back and sit through their arguing. But Father did say he had come to see me and he'll not see a lot of me if I hide in the kitchen. So I pick up the tray, brace myself and walk into the living room.

They abruptly stop talking when I come in. I place the tray on the centre table. I take two of the glasses and put one on the small table next to Father and one on the table next to Mummy. "Would you like some water?" I ask Father politely.

His face softens as he says with a smile, "Yes, thank you, Esi."

My mixed emotions make my hand shake a little as I pour the water into his glass. I offer Mummy some water, too. She nods and smiles tightly as I pour water into her glass.

Finally, I pour myself some water and sit down.

"So how are you, Esi?" Father asks after drinking some of his water.

"I'm fine ... Father." It's strange saying that word out loud. He seems to beam when I call him Father.

"It is good to see you. It has been too long."

"Why is that?" I ask before I have a chance to stop myself.

"Why is what?" Father looks puzzled.

With my anger now burning a hole in my chest, I look Father straight in the eye and ask, "Why is it that you've not seen me in so long?"

Father plays with the glass in his hand. "Um...um."

My anger will not allow me to look away from him. I want him to answer the question. I want to understand.

"Did you not know where I was when I was in Ghana?" I decide to ask.

Mummy snorts. "Of course, he knew."

"Yes, I did know," Father says quietly.

"Yet you never came to see me. How come?"

Father is silent for a moment before clearing his throat and saying, "Your mother and I did not break up amicably."

And so? I feel even angrier now. "What does that have to do with me?" I ask.

"Don't mind him," Mummy says. "Your father always has excuses for letting people down."

"Maggie, *you* are the reason why I stayed away. You didn't want me anywhere near you and Esi. You made that very clear on many occasions. You returned my letters and stopped your mother and sister from speaking to me. You pushed me away."

"Did you put up a fight?" Mummy glares at him, her voice raised. "You happily walked away. Where is the money for Esi's schooling, her clothing and all the other things she has needed? You have not contributed one jot to Esi's upbringing since the age of four. I've been doing it all."

"If you'd asked me, I would have contributed."

"Why should I have to ask you? Did you not know that you had to pay for the upkeep of your daughter?"

"You pushed me away, Maggie, and that is why I stayed away."

"*Why* did I push you away, Solomon? You betrayed me."

"And you wouldn't forgive me, Maggie. We could have moved past this if you were willing to forgive."

"So it is my fault, is it? Why don't you tell your daughter why I left?"

"It is not necessary to go through that now."

"I would like to know why you and Mummy broke up." I interrupt, needing to understand exactly what it is they're fighting about.

After a long silence, he says, in a quiet voice, "Your mother and I separated because I had a relationship with another woman."

"Why?" The question rushes out of my mouth.

"I don't know how it happened. It just happened. I'm not proud of it. The woman was someone who worked for me. She was always doing things for me and I let her. Then before I knew it, we were having a relationship. It did not last long and it did not mean anything."

"It did not mean anything?" Mummy erupts. "But you still did it when you knew that you were jeopardising your relationship with me."

"I didn't think that I was jeopardising my relationship with you. I didn't think you would find out. Moreover, plenty of marriages remain intact, even though the man has the odd affair. You're just too idealistic." Father drops his gaze as if he can't look Mummy in the eye.

She rolls her eyes and leans toward him. "Is it idealistic to expect the man who professes to love you and who has married you to be faithful? No, it is not, Solomon, and you know it. You are just making excuses."

"I have admitted that I made a mistake and I know that I hurt you. But you could have forgiven me, but you wouldn't, and you still haven't. How long will this go on for?"

"I don't have to forgive you or tell you when I will forgive you. *You* wronged *me*, remember?"

My head is thumping. Mummy and Father's arguing is making me more and more angry. It's like it is all about them. They are so engrossed in each other they don't realise what they have done to me. The things I have missed out on in my life.

"You are so selfish," I shout. My voice seems to echo around the room.

"Pardon?" Father says startled.

"What did you say?" says Mummy.

"I said you're selfish. You both don't see what you've done to me."

"Esi, you cannot speak to your parents like that," Father exclaims.

"Yes, you are being insolent, Esi." Mummy frowns at me.

"How is what I'm saying insolent?" My anger makes me bolder than I've ever been in my life. "I am stating a fact. It is true. You are both selfish."

"Is this how you have brought up our daughter? To be rude?" Father says to Mummy.

"*Don't bring yourself*, Solomon. Don't talk to me about raising our daughter when you've done nothing for her since she was four. How dare you!"

"I dare because she is still my daughter and I don't want her turning out badly. Look at what you and your family have done to her."

I just can't stand it anymore. "Be quiet!" I yell. "Look at you, so busy fighting and thinking about yourselves. It is clear now that you've given little thought to me."

122

Mummy and Father stare at me, shocked expressions on their faces.

But I can't stop the words from coming out of my mouth. "For so long, I would look and wonder why other children's fathers were there for them, but mine wasn't. Mummy didn't help by never speaking about you. That just made things worse."

"You haven't spoken to Esi about me?" Father says, looking accusingly at Mummy.

"Doesn't everyone deserve to know about their father?" My words rush out, preventing Mummy from responding to Father's accusation. "Ama's father died many years ago, but she knows a lot about him because Auntie Cissy talks to her about him, and her father's two brothers come to see her regularly. As for me, my father is alive, but I know little about him. For years, he has never come to see me. I don't know his parents – my own grandparents."

"Okay, Esi. That is enough," Mummy says sternly.

But I can't stop. I feel like I will explode if I stop talking.

"For years, I've wondered what could be so bad that my mother refuses to talk about my father and my father takes no interest in me? I've wondered if it was somehow my fault. But now I see that it's because you're selfish. You haven't thought about how your anger towards each other has affected me."

Father leaps up. "Esi, *wo mbu ade*. You are being disrespectful."

"Yes Esi," Mummy says. "You know better than to speak to your elders like that."

I realise then that they've not really heard what I've said to them. They are just concerned with my rudeness.

Suddenly, I have a strong urge to get out of the flat. I start running. I can hear them both shouting my name.

But I run out of the living room and down the stairs. Grabbing my coat from the coat stand in the hall, I open the front door and dash out.

27

Huffing and puffing, I keep running.

Further and further away from the flat.

Soon, I'm running down roads I've never been to before. When my legs feel like jelly and I'm struggling to breathe, I stop. I bend over and catch my breath. When I finally look up, I see that I'm standing in front of a park.

The park is surrounded by railings. Through the railings, I spot an unoccupied bench by a tree. Though the weather is chilly and overcast, the idea of sitting quietly for a while really appeals. Moving my tired legs slowly, I make my way to the bench and sit down. Through my jeans, I feel the cold of the wooden bench, but still, it feels good to sit. The large park has a play area in the far corner and two football pitches, on one of which a football match is being played.

But I'm not that interested in what is going on in the park. I've more pressing things to think about. Like how angry and disappointed I am with Mummy and Father. Why could I not have parents like Auntie Comfort and Uncle Kofi? They would never have treated Kojo the way my parents have treated me. Would Uncle Kofi have gone for years without seeing Kojo, even if Auntie Comfort had told him to stay away? I don't think so. No, I just have selfish parents!

I close my eyes and pray. *God, I know I'm complaining about Mummy and I promised that I wouldn't. But God, you need to show me how to handle how I'm feeling about my parents.*

"Well, if it isn't Essi?"

Those words jolt me out of my thoughts. I turn to see someone in tight blue jeans, a leather jacket, and black patent lace-up boots standing by the bench I'm sitting on. I look up and recognise the sneering face. It's Lisa. What is she doing here?

"What are you doing in the park on your lonesome?" scoffs Lisa. "No boyfriend today. Has he dumped you already? Is that why you're looking so sad?"

I don't want to deal with Lisa today of all days. I get up to walk away, but Lisa moves to stand directly in front of me, stopping me.

"Lisa, I'm going now. I don't want any trouble," I say, as I try to walk around her.

But Lisa moves with me. "You haven't answered my questions."

"I don't have to answer your questions, Lisa."

Over Lisa's shoulder, I can see a rowdy group of children approaching across the park. My breath catches as Lisa turns and waves at the group, who wave back at her. "Come over 'ere," she shouts to them.

What is this now? I'm going. I push past Lisa and start walking towards the park exit. But the next thing I know, there are children running up behind me and two teenage boys I don't recognise stand in front of me.

"Not so quick, Essi." Lisa's voice is bitter and hard.

"Lisa, I'm going home now," I say, not bothering to turn around. I push past the boys and try to get away, but more children move to stand in front of me, blocking my way and laughing at me.

126

"Did you think you could get away from me so easily?" says Lisa as she catches up with me. "No. Today, you have to listen to me. We're not at school and your boyfriend isn't here to protect you."

"I don't have a boyfriend, Lisa. I just want to go home now."

"You're not going anywhere until I've finished with you," says Lisa. "You got me bollocked at school. I had to do detention for the first time ever and my Mum came down on me like a ton of bricks afterwards. Now I have to sit with that git Hugh. Well, you're getting your comeuppance today."

"Get away from me," I shout.

"Nobody is here to help you today, Essi. I'm going to show you what I do to people who think they're better than me."

She pushes me towards a tall boy standing on the other side of me. He pushes me, too. Lisa pushes me again, as does the boy. I'm scared. What if they actually hurt me? I start to scream and scream.

"Leave her alone," a girl yells.

My heart racing with relief, I stop screaming but don't look away from Lisa, afraid she'll start shoving me again.

"What's it to you?" Lisa looks over my shoulder.

"Is that you, Lisa? What are you up to?"

"Well, if it isn't Karen. What are you wearing?"

Karen. Thank you, God. I knew you'd not abandoned me.

I push past the boy on my side and run as fast as I can towards Karen. She is standing with three other girls, looking a little sweaty in a blue and white football kit, long white football socks, and black football boots.

127

"Esi?" Karen holds out her hand to me when she sees me running to her. "Are you okay? Has Lisa hurt you?"

"She pushed me around, but she didn't hurt me," I say, as I reach her, my voice shaking. "Thank God you came when you did, though."

Karen looks furious. She turns to face Lisa, who is standing with her friends, smirking. "You're such a bully, Lisa. If you don't leave Esi alone, I'll tell Mr Herbert. Maybe this time, you'll be suspended from school. I'm sure your Mum would be thrilled with that."

"You wouldn't dare."

"I guess you'll find out."

"It'll be your word against mine."

"Yeah, and I know who he'll believe. I've also got witnesses," Karen says, pointing to the girls standing next to her.

"You're such a snitch." With her arms crossed, Lisa's still trying to look tough, but it's obvious from her expression that Karen has rattled her.

"Yes, I'll snitch if you don't leave Esi alone."

Lisa motions to the group of kids around her. "What if I get my friends to beat you up? That'll teach you not to be a snitch."

"I'll tell my mother."

Lisa walks up to Karen and stands in front of her - nose to nose. "Go on then. See if I care," she says. Karen doesn't flinch. "C'mon guys, let's show her how we deal with people who snitch," Lisa adds.

128

But even as I start to feel anxious as Lisa's friends approach, Karen says calmly, "You don't fool me, Lisa. I know you care. When I tell my mum, she will speak to your mum and you know what your mum will do to you." I watch in amazement as she keeps looking Lisa in the eye. Wow, Karen has got guts. She doesn't seem scared of Lisa at all.

Lisa's smirk slips, but she snarls, "Why am I wasting time talking to you?"

"I don't know. Sling your hook then," Karen replies.

"Make sure you keep Esi out of my way."

"Remember what I said. Leave Esi alone or else."

"Whatever," Lisa says, flicking her hand at Karen, before turning to her friends. "C'mon, let's go." Then they all walk off, heading across the park.

I can't take my eyes off Karen. I'm so impressed that she stared Lisa down.

"I'm alright," Karen says, as her three friends approach her concerned.

"Thanks for your help, Karen," I finally manage to say.

"No problem," Karen replies with a smile. "What are mates for?"

28

"How come you're here, anyway?" Karen asks.

"I had to get away from the flat and have space to think. Somehow, I ended up here. I'm not even sure where I am."

"You're in the park where I play football every Sunday morning. My house is just down there," Karen says pointing. "If you want, I can help you get home."

"That would be great." In truth, I don't want to be on my own. Lisa and her group might be waiting somewhere and I don't want to deal with another confrontation by myself. "But won't your parents be expecting you home?"

"It's no bother. I'll send Mum a message that I'll be late."

Karen turns to the girl standing next to her. "Amy, please ring my doorbell on your way home and tell Mum that I'm walking my friend Esi home."

"Okay. Will do. Catch you later." Amy and the other girls wave at us before heading for the park exit.

"C'mon then. Let me walk you home," Karen says. We follow the other girls out of the park, but head in the opposite direction.

"Don't worry about Lisa. I'll deal with her." There's a determined look on Karen's face.

"Thank you," I say, still feeling shaken by this morning's events.

"So how come you needed space to think, Esi?"

"I just needed to get away from my mother and father."

Karen looks surprised. "Father? I thought he wasn't around."

"He hasn't been around since I was four. But today, he turned up." It's strange saying it out loud.

"Blimey! That must have been a bit of a shock."

"You can say that again." I'll never forget seeing him standing in the doorway.

"Does he live in London, then?"

"No, he lives in Ghana, but he is in London with his mother. She has come for some medical treatment."

"His mother? You mean your grandmother?"

I shrug. "I don't know her. As far as I know, she's not seen me since I was four years old. So I don't think of her as my grandmother. The only grandmother I know is my mother's mother who I lived with before I came to London."

"I get ya. Did your father say why he is here?"

I summarise what Father said as best as I can.

"What did he say about why he hasn't come to see you for so long?"

I find that I don't want to say that he was with another woman. It feels ... shameful. So I don't. "He says he and Mummy didn't break up amicably and Mummy didn't want him anywhere near us."

"Is that it?" Karen frowns. "Oh, sorry Esi. Me and my gob."

"It's alright. I wasn't impressed either. With him or my mother. That's why I needed to get some air." I'm glad someone else understands.

"Don't blame you."

We walk for a while in silence.

"What has your father come to do?" Karen's question breaks the silence.

It gets me thinking. What had Father come to do? "I don't actually know."

"Hmm," Karen says.

It feels like we've been walking for a long time, down roads that don't look familiar. Thank God, Karen offered to help. Otherwise, I would have had no idea how to get back. "Are you sure your parents don't mind that you've not gone home straight after football?"

"No. Amy will give Mum the message and as long as I get home before two, it will be cool."

"What happens at two?"

"That's when we sit down to eat Sunday lunch. Mummy will still be cooking now and Dad will be asleep. He worked last night."

Karen's Dad is a manager at a warehouse. He is, as the English say, Hayes born and bred. But Karen says that when he met her mum, he went to live in Leeds with her for a few years before they returned to Hayes a couple of years after Karen was born. They have lived in Hayes ever since in the same house. So Hayes is home for Karen and she knows a lot of people here. I suppose that is how it was for me in Tesano. Here, I don't even know the people who live on either side of Mummy and Auntie Comfort's flats, never mind anybody else on my street. I've seen them but never said more than hello to them.

We turn a corner and suddenly I know where I am. We are on the main road. How did I manage to get so far? "I can find my way from here, if you want to go back," I say.

"I don't mind walking you home, Esi. I've got my bus pass on me. I'll get the bus back."

I smile and nod, happy Karen wants to stay with me.

"Have you decided what you'll do when you get back?" she asks.

"I've no idea. To tell you the truth, I'm not looking forward to facing Mummy and Father. I guess I'll have to play it by ear when I get there."

"They won't have had a clue where you were. They might be really worried."

I shrug. I know Karen is right, but I refuse to feel guilty.

"Mohammed lives down there," Karen announces suddenly, pointing to a road off the main road.

"Oh, I didn't know that."

"Mohammed hasn't seen his father for ages, either."

"How come?" I ask. I've never heard Mohammed talk about his father.

"He went missing in the Somali Civil war. Mohammed, his brother, and mother fled the war and came here as refugees five years ago."

I'm stunned. I've heard of refugees but had no idea Mohammed was one. "So, have they not heard from his father in all that time?"

"Mohammed says no."

"Wow, that's tough." Mohammed is so calm and thoughtful. You would never know that he had been through something as bad as Karen has just described. My respect for him goes up a notch. He has it worse than me, but I don't see him complaining. At least my father has come to see me and I know he's alive. Maybe I shouldn't be feeling so sorry for myself.

I can now see the turning onto my road. "Karen, my flat is just around the corner. I think you should go home now. I feel bad that you've come all this way because of me. Where can you get your bus from?"

"I can get this bus coming now."

I look up to see a bus trundling down the road, heading to the bus stop not far behind us.

"C'mon then, lets run and get you on it," I say.

We run to the bus stop and arrive just as the bus is stopping. I wait until Karen gets on and wave her off as the bus pulls away. I then resume walking to the flat and I'm just about to turn the corner when I hear my name being called out. I look behind me and see Kojo and Uncle Kofi running up to me.

"Where have you been? We have been looking all over for you," Uncle Kofi says, looking worried.

Now I feel guilty.

29

Opening the front door with my key, I walk in followed by Uncle Kofi and Kojo, who shuts the door behind us. Not eager to see Mummy and Father, I trudge up the stairs slowly. When I walk into the living room, I find Mummy sitting on her own on the sofa, looking sad. Guilt sweeps over me again. Only yesterday, I was thanking God and feeling relieved that Mummy was home and on the mend. Now I'm the reason why she is looking down.

Mummy looks up and relief lights up her face. She holds her hand out saying, "Oh good, Esi, you are back. Why did you run off like that?"

Saying nothing, I walk to Mummy.

"We found her just around the corner," Uncle Kofi explains when I don't speak. "She'd gotten lost but had found her way back."

"Thank God. I was so worried."

Putting my hand in Mummy's hand, I feel relieved. She seems more worried than angry. I'd been expecting screaming and shouting.

"Comfort and Solomon are on their way back," continues Uncle Kofi. "I called them when I saw Esi."

I freeze on hearing that. I'd not realised that Father was with Auntie Comfort. When I didn't see him in the living room, I assumed he'd gone. I dread to think what will happen when he comes back.

When Father returns with Auntie Comfort, I'm sitting at the dining table with Kojo. He looks awkward and doesn't say much. I don't' know what he and Mummy told Auntie Comfort and Uncle Kofi about what happened, but I suspect they didn't tell them that much.

Father thanks Uncle Kofi for finding me and nods at Mummy. He greets Kojo and then fixes his gaze on me, asking stiffly, "Are you okay?"

I nod but don't speak. I brace myself for a lecture but there is just uncomfortable silence. As Father goes to sit down on one of the armchairs, Auntie Comfort approaches me and gives me a big hug. "Running off is not the way to deal with problems, Esi," she admonishes, but her tone is gentle and her eyes are understanding.

"Comfort," says Uncle Kofi from the sofa next to Mummy, "I think it's time to leave Maggie, Esi, and Solomon to talk in peace."

"But Kofi, I wanted to sort out lunch for them before I went."

"No Comfort, you don't have to do that," Mummy says. "You have done so much already. Go and enjoy the rest of your Sunday."

"I want to do it, Maggie. It won't take long. It'll be too much for you and if I do it, then Esi won't have to. Kofi and Kojo can go first. I'll join them later."

"Alright," Uncle Kofi says, getting up. "Kojo and I will go down and start lunch. That way, when you get back, lunch will be ready."

"Really? You're cooking for me?" Auntie Comfort says to Uncle Kofi, laughing. "Eh, today is a really special day."

"Yes, it is. So don't be too long," Uncle Kofi replies with a smile. "Maggie, we'll see you soon. Try and take it easy." He gives Mummy a hug before getting up and walking over to Father, who stands up. "Good to meet you, Solomon," Uncle Kofi says simply. Father shakes his hand. Uncle Kofi then hugs me goodbye.

Kojo gets up. "See you tomorrow, Esi. I'll meet you at your front door at eight." Kojo's quiet presence has been comforting. Now that he is going, I almost want to ask him to stay, but I know that wouldn't be right.

I sigh. "Yeah, see you tomorrow morning."

Saying bye to Mummy and Father, Kojo follows Uncle Kofi out of the living room and soon the front door bangs shut.

"Well, I'll go and get lunch ready," Auntie Comfort announces.

"I'll help," I say, eager not to face Mummy and Father on my own.

"No Esi, you stay and speak to your parents," Auntie Comfort replies firmly.

As Auntie Comfort leaves, silence descends. I don't know what to say to Mummy and Father. So I sit, looking at my hands.

"Esi, *nti na woyεε anopa yi εkyerε sεn?* What was that about — you running away this morning?" I hear Mummy ask.

"I was upset," I mutter with a shrug.

"But running off like that? Worrying your Father and me, as well as Auntie Comfort, Uncle Kofi, and Kojo? When you didn't return and your father had walked around, but couldn't find you, I had to call Auntie Comfort. I couldn't go and look for you myself. Auntie Comfort, Uncle Kofi, and Kojo came rushing back from church and went out with your father to look for you. All this trouble."

As Mummy goes on and on, the burning feeling of anger returns. Doesn't she remember what was going on before I ran out? Why is she acting like I ran out for no good reason?

But still, I don't want to argue with Mummy. She is recuperating, and I don't want her health to get worse. So I swallow the words that want to come out.

"Yes, you have caused a lot of worry, Esi," I hear Father say.

Who is he to tell me that? He saunters into my life after years of ignoring me and now he wants to tell me off. "Well, you have caused *me* a lot of worry," I snarl quietly.

There is silence.

Father clears his throat. "Clearly you are angry, Esi," he says, his voice sounding gruff. "I want to make amends."

"How, exactly?" I ask, remembering Karen's question. "What have you come back to do?"

"I have come back to support you and your mother."

"How?"

"Esi, your mother may not have told you this, but you have to speak respectfully to your parents."

"Even when you haven't earned the respect?" The thought comes out of my mouth so fast I'm not able to stop it.

"Heh Esi, your mother and her family have really not taught you any manners."

"At least my mother and her family have taken care of me. What have you and your family done?" I retort angrily.

"Esi, that is enough," says Mummy, although she doesn't look angry.

I bite my tongue, but my anger still burns.

Suddenly Nana's voice is in my head, telling me, as she has done many times before, "Tↄ wo bo ase. Exercise patience." But I know I'll not be able to do that sitting here.

"Excuse me," I say, getting up abruptly.

I rush out of the living room. I hear Mummy calling me to come back, but I hurry to my bedroom, shutting the door behind me. I stay leaning against it, waiting for someone to come and try to open it. This is not how I imagined meeting my father. I had pictured being really happy, not angry and disappointed.

Father says he came back because Auntie Mary told his mother about Mummy's accident, but Auntie Mary knew that I was living with Auntie Comfort so surely she would have told Father's mother that, too. How come Father didn't come and see me there? Is the truth that he really only came back for Mummy?

"Esi?" I hear a voice on the other side of the door. "It's Auntie Comfort. Are you okay?"

"Yes Auntie, I'm alright."

"Come and have some lunch. I have put food on the table."

"I'm not hungry, Auntie." The thought of sitting across from Mummy and Father and trying to eat makes my stomach churn.

"I know you are upset Esi, but you still have to eat."

"I'm not hungry now. Maybe later. Please."

"Okay, my dear."

Then, after a moment, I hear her quietly say, "Esi, give your parents a chance. Things may seem bad now, but with God's grace, it will improve. You know you can always come and speak to me. I'll be happy to help."

Her kind words bring tears to my eyes. "Thanks, Auntie Comfort." Then I hear her walking away.

With my anger turning into an aching feeling inside, I walk to my bed and lie down under my duvet. The warmth of the duvet is soothing. I close my eyes and curl up like a ball, hoping to shut everything out.

30

Eyes drift open.

Darkness.

16.50 glows on my watch.

Gosh, I must have fallen asleep.

Is Father still here?

Hesitantly, I get out of bed and open my bedroom door, sticking my head out. The living room door is shut, but there is light shining out from under the door.

I venture out, walking gingerly towards the living room. As I get closer, I can hear a hum of voices. Maybe Father is still here. So what do I do now? Do I go in or go back to my room?

C'mon, Esi, go in, says a loud voice in my head. *You might regret it if you don't.*

Still unsure, I put my hand on the handle of the living room door and push it open.

Silence greets me. Mummy and Father are in the living room, but seated next to Father is an unfamiliar, elderly, frail, black woman dressed in a smart white blouse and blue skirt. There is no sign of Auntie Comfort. She must have gone home already.

"Esi, did you have a good rest?" Mummy says with a tentative smile, her hand outstretched as if beckoning me to come to her. I nod and start to walk towards her.

"Esi," Father then says, making me stop. "Come and meet your grandmother. She came by cab to see you but you'd fallen asleep."

Standing still, I stare at the old woman smiling at me. Is this really Father's mother? Struggling to get my head around it, I turn to Mummy. "Is this Father's mother?"

"Yes, Esi," Mummy replies cautiously. "Go and say hello."

My mind whirling, I walk over to Father's mother. I try to see any resemblance between her and me. It is hard to tell. She doesn't look well. Her skin has a greyish hue. Her face looks drawn and tired. Her visible skin is hanging off her as if she has lost a lot of weight.

"Yes, Esi, I am your grandma Asantewa. I have prayed for a long time that we would meet. I am really happy that I have managed to see you today."

She puts her hand out. As I shake her hand, it feels bony and frail.

"You are beautiful," she says, with a sad-looking smile.

Anger sweeps over me at her words.

"Until a few months ago, I was living with Nana Nancy in Ghana. I'm sure you knew where I was. Yet you never called me, came to see me or even wrote to me. What stopped you?" The words rush out.

"Not again. Esi, you cannot speak to your grandmother like that!" Father exclaims.

"Solomon, it is fine," Nana Asantewa says. "Let her speak. You are angry, Esi, and you have every right to be. It is true that Solomon, Sam, and I have treated you badly."

I stand in stunned silence. On the one hand, I'm wondering who Sam is, but more than that, I cannot believe that Father's mother has just apologised to me. After all these years! What has brought this on?

"Pride is a terrible thing, Esi," continues Nana Asantewa. "We, the Addo family, have been a proud family for far too long. I see that with absolute clarity now, but it has taken me facing death to realise it."

My mind goes into overdrive. Did she say she is facing death? What does she mean by that?

She obviously sees my confusion. "Yes, unfortunately, I have got cancer and the prognosis is not good."

This calm statement of fact is too much to take in. Silently I turn and go to Mummy, who clasps my hand in hers tightly.

"Mama Asantewa, I am really sorry to hear your news," Mummy says. "But this is not a good way to break the news to Esi. She is a child."

"Yes, Maggie. Of course, you are right."

I slump onto Mummy's armrest, digesting what Nana Asantewa has said.

Suddenly, I feel angry again.

"So is it because you are dying that you have come to find me?" I burst out. "If you were not dying, would I still not be worth contacting?"

"Esi! I insist that you watch how you speak to your grandmother." Father leaps to his feet, outrage on his face.

"I said leave her alone, Solomon," Nana Asantewa says, gesturing for Father to sit down. "Yes, Esi, I have to admit that facing death has given me the urgency to fix the wrongs that I have done. I know that the way I have treated you is wrong. You are my only grandchild, Esi. I will not be able to end my life in peace if I have not managed to make peace with you."

"You've only spoken about me. What about Mummy? What about the wrong done to her?" I retort, remembering Father's admission this morning.

Nana Asantewa looks at Father. "Solomon, what do you have to say to Esi?"

"That is a matter for Maggie and me. I cannot discuss adult matters with Esi." Father looks adamant, his jaw clenched.

Nana Asantewa gives him a stern look. "Solomon, we are here to clear the air," she says. "You *do* owe your child an explanation as to why you and her mother are no longer together."

"I already told Esi this morning," Father says. "I am not going over it again."

But Nana Asantewa carries on. "So tell them why you chose to have a relationship with someone else when you had made a commitment to Maggie."

Next to me, Mummy gazes at Father. Father squirms. He looks at Nana Asantewa, who nods as if to say go on.

I'm surprised by the interaction between Father and Nana Asantewa. He acts the big man, but with his mother, he still acts like a child.

"I would like to know," Mummy pipes up.

"You are enjoying this, aren't you? Watching me suffer!" Father retorts, rather petulantly.

"No, I am not, Solomon." Mummy sounds calm now, not angry like before. "I can see now that I was so angry at your betrayal that I allowed things to remain unsaid to protect myself from even more hurt. But that has been counterproductive. Because, in actual fact, I've struggled to move on." The last bit is said as if it's just dawning on her.

"It must be uncomfortable, seeing your parents talking like this," Nana Asantewa says. I turn to find her eyes on me. I nod.

"In truth, I feel partly responsible," she continues. "You see, Solomon's father had affairs too, but I decided to put up with them and stay in the marriage. I did not want to jeopardise my family and I wanted to stay married. I liked being Mrs Addo. I did not think that Solomon knew about his father's affairs but now I wonder, Solomon, if you did know."

Father nods, his eyes fixed on her.

"I did you a disservice then. It seems that because I stayed married to your father, you learnt that having an affair whilst married is not a big deal. But of course, it is. I felt I had too much to lose by leaving, but that didn't mean that I didn't feel hurt and betrayed by what your father did. A part of me died every time I became aware that Sam was having an affair, and my respect for him diminished significantly. Yes, your father and I are still married, but barely. We live virtually separate lives now. In the end, his affairs killed the marriage. He was wrong, and you were too."

Nana Asantewa falls silent. I try and take in everything I've heard. I now know that Sam is my Grandad. Father is still looking at Nana Asantewa intently. I think he has learnt something new today about his mother and father. It would seem that the Addo family, from whom I've felt excluded for so long, are far from the perfect family.

Nana Asantewa turns to me. "Maybe what I have said is not for children's ears, Esi, but I may not be around to tell you later, so that is why I decided to say what I said in your presence. I hope you learn from it and do not repeat the same mistakes."

Father sighs dramatically. "Maggie and I are not like you and Dad. I didn't have multiple affairs whilst we were together. I only had one affair."

"Solomon, stop talking nonsense." Nana Asantewa sounds irritated. "You threw away your marriage after you had fought so hard to marry Maggie. You threw away your chance to be a better father to Esi than your father was to you. Just one affair...what nonsense. You shouldn't have had any. That is what I will never understand. Did you get scared? Did the responsibility of being a husband and a father scare you?"

Nana Asantewa must have hit on something because Father becomes fidgety, although he doesn't answer her question immediately. Eventually, with all of us staring at him, he clears his throat. "I was scared of being a father," he admits. "When Maggie told me she was pregnant, it just felt too soon. I was not ready. Maggie was overjoyed about us having a baby so I never told her about my fear, but it never left me. Even after Esi was born, I still found it hard to come to terms with being a father. I found it easier to stay longer at work or go out drinking with my mates so that I could spend as little time as possible at home. That way, I could avoid having to deal with being a father. This new lifestyle created arguments between Maggie and me. This made me want to spend even less time at home. Then I had the affair." He pauses before quietly saying, "I'm not proud of it."

Silence descends.

146

It dawns on me that with all that I've learnt about Father today, I somehow don't feel as angry with him. In fact, I feel sorry for him. It's clear that Father has been immature. It doesn't excuse how he has treated me, but at least I understand him better now.

Mummy breaks the silence. "Thank you for being honest, Solomon. You have confirmed things that I have wondered about. Finally, I may be able to move on."

"What do you mean, move on?" Father asks tersely.

"This is not the best time to talk about this, but we do need to formally end things between us."

Father looks unhappy and is about to say something when Nana Asantewa speaks up.

"You and Solomon have to continue that conversation on your own, Maggie. I am sure that Esi has heard enough. Um, I am hoping that you will agree, Maggie, to you and Esi coming to visit me and Solomon in my serviced flat. I am going to be here for another ten days before returning to Ghana."

"Thank you for inviting us," Mummy says carefully, after a moment's hesitation. "But as you can see, my leg is in a cast and I am still recuperating following my accident, so it would be difficult for me to travel there."

"I can come and get you and Esi," Father offers quickly. "I have hired a car for the time I'm here. I would be happy to come and pick you up."

His comments hang in the air as a look passes between him and Mummy.

There is a fleeting expression on Mummy's face before, with a nod, she says quietly, "Okay."

"I will call and agree the time to pick you up," Father says, looking happy.

"On the subject of phone calls," begins Nana Asantewa, "I would appreciate it if you would let me and Solomon call regularly. I have allowed my anger about you leaving Solomon to cloud my judgement for so long that it has stopped me from contacting Esi. It is by far the worst thing that I have done in my life. But now with the limited time I have left, it would make me so happy to get to know Esi better. I hope you will find it in your heart to allow me to call."

I look at Nana Asantewa. Although my brain is telling me not to let her off too easily, my heart has warmed to her and I do want to get to know this plucky, straight-talking woman.

"It's okay to call," I say, as Mummy smiles up at me nodding.

Nana Asantewa's face crumples and she begins to cry. "Bless you, Esi. You have delighted an old woman," she says. When she stretches her hand out to me, I walk to her and put my hand in hers. Suddenly, with a strength that belies her frailty, Nana Asantewa pulls me towards her for a tight embrace. As she lets me go, she frames my face with her bony hands and looks into my eyes.

"I love you, Esi Asantewa. I hope one day you can find it in your heart to love me too."

She plants a heartfelt kiss on my forehead.

Tears are running down my face now. My whole life I've wanted to be acknowledged by Father's family. So Nana Asantewa telling me that she loves me is overwhelming.

Nana Asantewa turns her gaze to Mummy. "Maggie, you and your family have done such a great job with Esi. You should be proud.

She's strong and she speaks her mind. There's nothing wrong with that."

"I am proud of Esi."

"That is good. Please, Maggie, I hope you will accept my apologies for not being the mother-in-law you deserved and allow me to make amends. I would really like to contribute to Esi's upkeep."

Mother raises her eyebrows. "Thank you for the apology, Mama Asantewa. You don't have to contribute to Esi's upkeep. I manage."

"I can see that you manage, Maggie, but please let a dying woman have her final wish. I would really like to help so that when I am dead, Esi will one day look back on me with fond thoughts."

This sets off more tears. Even Father wipes his tears away as he gazes at his mother. I ask myself why I am feeling so emotional over someone who has ignored me most of my life. I realise that my tears are partly because of my sadness about what may have been had I had a relationship with Nana Asantewa all my life. From what I have seen of her today, I like her. I even wonder if some of my traits have been inherited from her.

Mummy agrees to let Nana Asantewa contribute — how could she not?

With that, Nana Asantewa places her hands on her knees and leans forward. "Solomon and I will get going. I am getting a bit tired now." She gets up carefully, her frailty clearly evident as she leans on Father. "It has been wonderful spending time with you."

Nana Asantewa and Father proceed to walk slowly to the landing and down the stairs. I walk behind with Mummy. But with her crutches, Mummy only walks as far as the top of the stairs. I continue down the stairs, following Nana Asantewa and Father.

I open the front door. As they walk out, Nana Asantewa kisses my cheek. "Goodnight, my dear."

Father exchanges a look with Mummy. "See you on Saturday," he says with a slight smile before awkwardly giving me a hug. Though Father's hug is brief, it is the first hug I remember from him.

As he walks away holding Nana Asantewa's arm, I shut the front door, my heart beating fast as so many emotions race through my body. What a day it has been today.

31

"What would you like, love?" asks the red-haired dinner lady.

I look at the food on offer in the stainless-steel containers. Apart from the rice and vegetables, they look unrecognisable.

"What is there?" I ask.

The dinner lady gives me an exasperated look. "You can either have shepherd's pie," she points to the container with a brown indistinguishable mass covered by a layer of mashed potato, "with vegetables, or vegetable curry," now she points to a container full of vegetables in a strange greeny-brown sauce, "with rice."

I don't really want either dish, but having not brought any packed lunch today, I have to eat something. Yesterday, Savaan, Kojo, Karen, Mohammed, and I decided that today we were going to stay in the warmth of the canteen at lunchtime and have a hot meal. It's been freezing outside since we got back to school following the half term, and three days in, we were fed up of eating our packed lunches outside in the cold.

I look at the food again. "Curry and rice, please." It looks marginally better than the shepherd's pie. The lady slaps the food onto the plate and gestures. "Pudding's over there, love."

Moving along the counter, the second, younger dinner lady asks, "Cake and custard?"

I look closely at the cake. Growing up with Nana's cakes, it's hard not to compare all other cakes to hers and find them wanting. The

151

last time I had cake at the canteen, it was by far the worst cake I'd ever eaten.

"Yoghurt, please," I say to the dinner lady, deciding that was the safer choice. As I leave the serving counter with my food, I look around the busy canteen to see if I can spot the others. I see Karen waving at me and wave back. She points to a seat next to her and mouths, "This is yours." I smile, mouthing back, "Thanks."

Having paid for my food, I start to walk towards the table. But getting up, from a table I'm about to walk past, are Lisa and her friends. *Oh no!* Karen told me on Monday that she'd spoken to her Mum about what happened in the park on Sunday and her Mum had decided to speak to Lisa's Mum about it. Karen assured me that Lisa wouldn't bother me anymore.

I said, "That's what Mr Herbert said the last time too, but you saw what Lisa was doing to me in the park."

"I promise you Lisa won't bother you now. She's more scared of her Mum than she is of Mr Herbert. If her Mum was to hear Lisa had done something she'd told her not to do, she'd knock Lisa's block off."

"She sounds a bit scary," I said.

"She is, believe me." Karen grinned.

Still, since coming back to school after the half term, I've been keeping out of Lisa's way. Until now.

I hold on tight to my tray, bracing myself for a confrontation. Lisa and her friends start to walk towards me and I can feel my heart beating faster.

Lisa comes up to me but then walks past with her friends in tow. Her friends snigger loudly as they go past, clearly for my benefit, but I don't care. Lisa left me alone. Karen was right. I'm so relieved.

"Told you she wouldn't bother you," Karen says to me, as soon as I get to the table.

"I can't thank you enough, Karen." I sit down between her and Savaan. "You've done me such a big favour. Lisa has been the bane of my life since I started here."

"Forget about her and enjoy your lunch," says Mohammed from the other side of the table. "Though, since you've chosen the same food I did, that may not be possible. This curry is ... strange."

Kojo and Karen make noises in agreement. They are also eating the curry and rice.

"How's the shepherd's pie?" Kojo asks Savaan, who is the only one eating it. Since coming back from half term, Savaan has spent every break with us and it feels like he's become the new member of our little group of friends.

Savaan gives a thumbs up. "Good. British food is exotic to me. I only get to eat it at school. At home, my mother just cooks Bangladeshi dishes. Besides, I couldn't eat that curry — it doesn't look like any curry I know."

"Great, Savaan," says Kojo. "That really makes us want to eat it!"

With my tummy starting to rumble, I take a tentative forkful and start to eat. The curry doesn't taste awful, just not like anything I've tasted before.

The hot school lunches at Hayes Road School are so different from the school meals served by Madame Serwah, the school cook at Tesano International. I always looked forward to lunch when I was there. Apart from Nana, I swear, she made the best jollof rice and chicken I'd ever eaten. Here, if I had to eat this food every lunchtime, I would lose weight. Definitely, from now on, I will stick to my packed lunches.

"How is your Mum?" Mohammed asks, looking at me.

"She's getting there," I say. "On Monday, she was really tired and spent a lot of time in bed. But yesterday, when I got home, she was in the kitchen hobbling around cooking dinner, which was a surprise because Mummy doesn't like to cook."

"She's probably cooking to stop being bored," Kojo suggests. "She's stuck in the flat all day."

"True," I say, thinking Mummy must have been *really* bored to have been driven to cook.

"And what's happening with your Dad?" Savaan asks.

I've been telling him and the others about what's been going on with Father and Nana Asantewa. It's been a relief having people to talk to about the confusion I feel.

"He and Nana Asantewa called last night. He'll be picking Mummy and me up to have lunch with them on Saturday."

"That's good, isn't it?" says Karen.

"Yeah, and he said more to me last night than he did on Monday."

"I think he was nervous on Monday that you'd get into a strop like you did on Sunday," says Karen between mouthfuls.

"Esi was entitled to be angry with him," Kojo says.

"I know that but maybe he didn't know how to handle it."

"Maybe," I say, moving my food around my plate.

"You're lucky, Esi," says Mohammed, looking pensive and sad.

154

Concerned, we all fall silent.

"You alright, mate?" Kojo asks gently.

"Yeah. Just miss my Dad a lot," Mohammed replies quietly. "I'd be over the moon if he turned up at my doorstep, but that's not likely to happen."

Kojo puts his arm around Mohammed and gives him a squeeze.

Remembering what Karen told me about Mohammed's father, I feel guilty that by talking about my dad, I'd made him feel sad.

Next to me, Savaan looks confused. Being the newest member of our group, he hasn't heard that Mohammed's Dad is missing.

"What happened to your father?" he asks, before adding hastily, "Only if you want to talk about it."

"I'll talk about it," says Mohammed, in a quiet voice. "My mother had to flee with me and my brother from our home in Mogadishu, as she was warned that our lives were in danger. My father had travelled to our hometown to help my grandmother so he wasn't with us, but he spoke to Mummy on the phone and told her to go ahead. He got people to help us escape to Ethiopia. He was meant to follow. We ended up in a refugee camp and though Mummy was able to call my Father to tell him where we were, he never came. Then, some days later, she could no longer reach him. Since then we haven't heard from him and don't know where he is."

"I'm so sorry," says Savaan, clearly taken aback.

"Sorry, Mohammed," I say too, shocked and saddened. Hearing directly from him, as opposed to Karen, what had happened to him and his family makes it far more real.

"For a while, Mummy didn't want to leave the refugee camp just in case my father turned up. But when the opportunity to move to

155

the UK came, she decided to take it, because she knew that my father would have wanted her to give me and my brother a future. When we got to the UK, Mum registered my Dad's details with the Red Cross, who help find family members missing in war."

We all sit in silence looking at Mohammed. It seems that none of us is sure of what to say.

"You can't give up hope, Mohammed," says Kojo finally. "You've told me about other Somali families reunited with relatives who've been missing for ages. So you know it can happen."

"*Inshallah*," Mohammed says.

"Your Dad would be so proud of you if he could see you now," Kojo continues. "You've got your head screwed on and you're definitely the smartest one amongst us."

"Kojo, don't go all mushy on me," says Mohammed with a smile and watery eyes.

"I'll get mushy if I want to." Kojo gives him a gentle push, smiling.

"Yeah, let him," says Karen. "It may be a long time before we see his sensitive side again."

That makes us all laugh.

"Sorry guys, I didn't mean to bring you down," Mohammed says.

"Don't be daft," Karen replies and touches his hand. "You've got nothing to apologise for."

"Esi, I wanted to say ..." Mohammed looks at me with a serious expression. "I think ... since your Dad has admitted that he has done wrong, you should accept it and forgive him. Then make the most of him and his mother being back in your life."

Nodding, I say, "You're right, Mohammed."

As I sit watching him, Kojo, Karen, and Savaan, I get a warm feeling inside and start to smile. I admire each of them. They've all helped me in some way and I feel really lucky to call them friends.

32

Father and Mummy.

Side by side.

Mummy, wearing a green and white dress and smart beige coat, is sitting in the passenger seat with her plaits lying loose and makeup on.

Father, driving, appears to have made a special effort too in his brown blazer, white shirt, and black trousers.

Sitting in the back seat of the rented Ford Fiesta, I've spent most of the journey watching them. We're heading to the serviced flat to see Nana Asantewa and have lunch. Though there have been some long periods of silence, Mummy and Father have been talking and smiling at each other, sometimes bringing me into their conversation. Father even surprised me by telling me I look pretty in my red dress, with my hair pulled into a bunch.

This probably shouldn't feel like a big deal, but it really does.

In such a short time, Mummy and Father's relationship seems to have progressed. On Monday and Tuesday, Mummy wouldn't even speak to Father when he called, telling me to give him some excuse like she was in the bathroom. That made me uncomfortable, as she was asking me to lie to him.

But on Wednesday, inspired by what Mohammed said at lunchtime, I decided that Mummy should forgive Father, but that was never going to happen if she refused to speak to him. So when the phone rang at seven-thirty that evening, the time that Father had called the two previous nights, I picked up the phone and gave it to Mummy before leaving the living room, in spite of her telling me to stay. Then, I hovered out of sight by the living room door and waited. Mummy held the phone for a while before finally speaking, her voice sounding strained. When it was clear that she was talking to Father, I went into the kitchen to wash up the dinner stuff.

When I finished and stepped back out of the kitchen, I was surprised to see Mummy still on the phone. I retreated to my room and it was quite a while before I heard Mummy shouting out my name. Back in the living room, she handed me the phone, saying Father wanted to talk to me. As I spoke to him, I noticed that he sounded much happier than he had the previous times he'd spoken to me.

Mummy spoke to Father on Thursday evening, again for a long time.

Something had definitely changed.

Then on Friday, Mummy did something out of the blue.

When school finished, I was walking to meet Kojo to go home when I saw Mrs Pier walking quickly towards me.

"Ah Essi," she said when she caught up with me. "Can I see you for a moment in my office?"

"Yes Mrs Pier," I said, my heart sinking.

"It won't take long and then you can go home. Don't worry. Nothing is wrong," she added with a smile.

When we entered her office, we sat down on the two hard-backed chairs in front of her desk.

"Esi," she said, "Your mother came to see me this morning."

"She did?" I replied, surprised. I knew Mummy was going to hospital for a check-up with Auntie Comfort, but I had no idea she was planning to come to school as well.

"She said you've been feeling frustrated at school and you're worried about the GCSEs you think you're going to be allowed to do."

I was stunned. I'd given up on Mummy coming to school to speak about this.

"Your mother brought in your reports and records from your previous school. It would have been useful to have received this when you first arrived," said Mrs Pier.

"What? But Mummy said you said you didn't need them."

"I think there's been some misunderstanding. Anyway, I've had a look. It's clear that, academically, you were doing well there. Of course, this is a different country and education system ..."

It's on the tip of my tongue to tell Mrs Pier that Tesano International followed the English curriculum, so though it was in a different country, it was the same education system. But I chose to stay silent, not wanting to argue and risk antagonising her.

"I've shared the information your mother brought in with your teachers," Mrs Pier continued. "After some discussion, we've agreed that the work you've done here so far tallies with the information from your previous school, so we're prepared to move you up a set from Monday."

I couldn't believe my ears. "Thank you so much, Mrs Pier," I said, elated.

When I got home, I thanked Mummy and told her what Mrs Pier had said. She was pleased and tried to make out that she was always going to go to the school. But I know that something changed for her to go.

Her touchy-feeliness towards me since coming out of hospital hasn't stopped. As well as holding my hand quite a lot, she now gives me a hug before I go to school and when I get home. She's also been asking me more about school and my friends.

On Friday, sitting next to her as we watched TV, I felt like telling her about Lisa for the first time. She listened quietly as I told her about what Lisa had done at school and in the park. In the end, she said, "Esi, I wish you'd told me about this earlier. Please don't keep something like this to yourself again."

"Okay Mummy," I said, suddenly felt lighter, like a weight had been lifted off my shoulders. "The thing I don't understand is why she's been acting the way she has towards me."

"Esi, sometimes people don't know how to deal with someone who looks and acts differently to them, so they try and put that person down. But you don't have to put up with it. You should always tell because their thinking has to be challenged. Do you want me to talk to the school about her?"

"There's no need. Karen has sorted it out and Mr Herbert knows about her."

"I'm glad, Esi, that you've made good friends who help you out when you haven't been here that long. But next time, let me know straight away when you are facing problems."

"Alright Mummy, I will." The tight hug that followed made me feel warm and tingling inside.

When Father called later that night, I spoke to him before giving Mummy the phone. She hobbled slowly with the phone to her room to speak to him. She was in there for ages. Then I heard her calling me.

When I entered her bedroom, she was sitting on her bed. She handed me the phone, saying, "Auntie Cissy wants to say hello."

Surprised, I took the phone and spoke to Auntie Cissy. As we spoke, it emerged that Mummy had called her straight after speaking with Father. I wondered why but knew it would be rude to ask.

Speaking to Auntie Cissy meant I could also speak to Ama. I walked out of Mummy's room with the phone when Ama came on, and I flopped onto my bed while we talked. I told her all that had happened since I'd last spoken to her on Saturday.

"Oh, how I wish I had been there." Ama said, before adding, "For Auntie Maggie to have gone from not even wanting to talk about your father to having long conversations with him, I think she still has a soft spot for him."

Looking at Mummy and Father now, as we ride to the flat, I think that Ama may have put her finger on it.

Nana Nancy, when I spoke to her after Ama on Friday, proclaimed that God was answering her prayers. Mummy, instead of shying away as she had done for so long, was communicating with my father and my father was communicating with me. Nana said she would pray for God to continue leading the way. Though she said she never understood why Nana Asantewa hadn't kept in contact with me, she encouraged me to keep speaking to her. I was happy to hear that, as at the back of my mind, I'd been wondering if getting on with Nana Asantewa meant I was betraying Nana Nancy.

Sitting in the same car as Father, I'm surprised at how comfortable I feel and how he doesn't feel like a stranger anymore. I know much more about him, thanks to his daily calls. I know his age, forty, which is five years older than Mummy. He is Nana Asantewa and Grandad Sam's only son. He went to school in Ghana but went to university in London. From the way he talks about it, he got to know London well and had a good time here. But once he graduated from university, he chose to go back to Ghana to train to be a lawyer at the Ghana Bar. I get why he did that — there's no place quite like your own country. Father still lives in the same house in East Legon that he and Mummy shared when they were together.

I sit up when Father pulls into a small car park in front of a white block of flats in Harrow.

Soon we're walking alongside Father down a walkway with fancy wallpaper and plush carpet. Father stops when we get to a grey door with a number eleven on it. He pulls a key out of his pocket, opens the door, and stands back to let Mummy and me in first.

Stepping into the flat, it sinks in that Father and Nana Asantewa live in a different world from Mummy and I. Father told me this week that he owned his own law firm. I hadn't fully appreciated what that meant, but now it is clear. He must be rich. How else can he and Nana Asantewa come from Ghana and rent a flat like this in London? Living with Nana in Ghana and Mummy in London, I never felt poor, but I never felt rich either. I remember what Mummy said about Father not paying anything towards my upkeep since she left him and that irks me. Maybe if Father had paid for my upkeep, as it appears he can clearly afford to do, Mummy wouldn't have felt the need to come to work in London to earn more money and she and I would still be living in Ghana.

"Oh good, you're here." A happy looking Nana Asantewa emerges gingerly into the hall, interrupting my train of thought. She looks as frail as she did when I saw her last Sunday.

163

After hugging both Mummy and me, she leads us slowly into a living room furnished beautifully with cream furniture and sumptuous curtains.

Nana Asantewa and Father then set out to make Mummy and me comfortable. Nana Asantewa insists that Mummy sits on a particular armchair so that she can rest her leg on a footstool next to it. I sit on the sofa next to Mummy. Nana Asantewa comes to sit next to me. Father orders Chinese food for our lunch then brings us refreshment from the kitchen. As he serves us, his clumsiness suggests he's not used to serving others. I offer to help.

"No, just relax, Esi," he says firmly. "You're a guest."

So I sit back and marvel at this new experience of having my father serving me.

Nana Asantewa asks Father to bring over a large black holdall in the corner of the living room. From the holdall, she pulls out photo albums. "I brought these from Ghana on the off chance I would be able to show them to you." She enthusiastically opens each photo album and goes through it with me. I see numerous Addo family photos, including some of Father as a child. I see photos of Grandad Sam and see Father's resemblance to him. There are photos of a younger Nana Asantewa, who looks so much like me that I now understand why Ms Mary said what she did.

From the corner of my eye, I see Father pulling up a chair next to Mummy. Like in the car, they sit talking with intermittent periods of silence. They look like friends ... or even a couple. That fleeting thought has my heart beating fast.

When lunch arrives, Father lays it out on the small glass dining table in the corner of the room along with plates, cutlery, and glasses. He invites us to sit at the dining table, pushing Mummy's chair in after she sits down before sitting next to her. I sit next to Nana Asantewa on the other side of the dining table. Throughout lunch, my earlier fleeting thought stays on my mind as I watch Mummy and Father. The food we eat is delicious but different from the Chinese food I'd eaten in Ghana. Even the fried rice is not like the Ghana fried rice I know.

Later, when Mummy and I are about to leave to go back to our flat, Nana Asantewa tells me to take the holdall full of photo albums.

"These are things to remember me and the Addo family by, Esi," she says, as she kisses me goodbye.

There is something final about Nana Asantewa's words. I walk away with a feeling of dread.

33

Wednesday 8th November 2000.

The day Nana Asantewa died.

Aged sixty-eight.

Not in Ghana, but in a London hospital near Harrow.

Her death has hit me hard.

I've been thinking about it and wondering why. But now I realise it's because she is the only person I've known who has died ... and I feel cheated. Cheated by the short time I had with her when it could have been so much longer.

At least I got to know her. It means a lot to me that I have known both my grandmothers, for in their own way they've both shaped me. Nana Nancy has given me love and security most of my life, and Nana Asantewa helped bring Father back into my life. Through her, I learnt a lot about the Addo family.

Today, thoughts of the Addo family are on my mind as I stand with Mummy, both of us dressed in black, outside the grey front door of the serviced flat. In a moment, I'll be meeting Grandad Sam. He flew in from Ghana on the day that Nana Asantewa died and is staying with Father at the flat. Mummy and I have come by minicab for the family meeting following Nana Asantewa's death.

When Father opens the door, I am overwhelmed by the sense of déjà vu. It was only last Saturday that I stood here with him and Mummy about to have lunch with Nana Asantewa. It is hard to take that a week later, we are back at the flat, but Nana Asantewa is dead.

Father stands in his black shirt and trousers, the strain and sorrow of the last few days evident on his face. He and Mummy look at each other for quite a while before Mummy reaches out and Father steps forward to hug her. I feel emotional as I watch them, as it's the first time I've seen them hug. When Mummy finally walks into the flat, I give Father a tearful embrace. He holds me tight as we stand united in grief for Nana Asantewa. When Father lets me go, he gazes at me with tears in his eyes, saying, "Thank you, Esi, I needed that." Taking out a handkerchief to dab his eyes, he holds my hand and ushers me into the living room with Mummy.

The living room is full of people. Some seated, but many standing. Most of the women are dressed in black *kaba* and *sleet* with their hair covered by black scarves. The men are either in black suits or black shirts and black trousers.

"Who are all these people?" I ask.

Father scans the room, as he says, "They are relatives and a few family friends who live in London."

Really! Not so long ago, I thought I was on my own in London. Now it turns out I had all these relatives that I didn't know anything about.

Amidst the throng of people, I spot Grandad Sam. In the flesh, the similarity between Father and him is undeniable, though Grandad Sam's hair is now completely grey. Dressed in a black suit, he is seated quietly in an armchair, looking grief-stricken. Father leads me and Mummy to him. Grandad Sam remains seated as he shakes Mummy's hand and accepts her condolences. Then he catches sight of me. His face lights up, as he exclaims, "God almighty! Asantewa, is that you? Have you come back?"

Startled, I realise that he thinks that I am Nana Asantewa. I say, "No, I'm Esi."

"Asantewa, do not play games with me. I can see that it is—"

"Dad, this is Esi, your granddaughter." Father puts his hand on Grandad's shoulder to get his attention.

There is a moment of hush as everyone in the room falls silent. Grandad Sam stares intently at my face. "Well, well," he eventually says softly. "Asantewa told me that she had really enjoyed the time she had spent with you, Esi, but she failed to tell me that you were her spitting image. Please, humour me and sit down beside me," he says, pointing to the chair next to him. As I sit down, Father grabs another chair and puts it down on my right for Mummy.

Throughout the family meeting, I sit next to Grandad Sam. As people take turns talking about Nana Asantewa and sharing their memories of her, I watch him. From time to time he sobs, sometimes quietly and other times quite loudly. He doesn't say much, just turns from time to time and gazes at me. He looks like a broken man, very different from the man Nana Asantewa spoke to me about.

She told me that she and Grandad Sam were childhood sweethearts from Kumasi. They got married in their twenties and lived in Legon, Accra where Grandad Sam worked as an Economics lecturer at the University of Ghana. He had studied at the LSE in London on scholarship before returning to Ghana to work as a lecturer. Nana Asantewa studied English at Legon and then worked at the University as an English lecturer. Father was born whilst Grandad Sam and Nana Asantewa lived and worked at Legon.

Nana Asantewa said that whilst at Legon, Grandad Sam got more and more involved in politics, eventually giving up his job as a lecturer to become an economic adviser to the then governing party. Many years later, he became the Finance Minister. When he was Minister, Nana Asantewa gradually gave up lecturing to support him.

According to her, politics changed Grandad. I remember her saying, "Sam used to be sober and hardworking. A quiet man who appreciated what he had. But through politics, he developed a taste for the high life, only wanting the best that money could buy. He started laughing *hee hee hee* like a big man. When women began paying him attention, it went straight to his head and the affairs began." She paused then for a while before saying quietly, "It got to a point where I would look at him and not see the man I married. It was like I was married to a completely different person, one I did not particularly like."

Despite Nana Asantewa's words, looking at Grandad Sam now, I feel sorry for him. He never got to say goodbye to Nana Asantewa. She passed away whilst he was on the flight from Ghana to London.

At least I managed to say goodbye. That Wednesday, I was at school when Mrs Pier came to get me from Maths.

She told me to bring my bag and coat. Surprised, I quickly went to get my things before following her to the school reception. Mummy was waiting for me. Before I could say anything, she told me that Nana Asantewa had been rushed to the hospital early that morning and that Father had called to say that Nana Asantewa was asking for us. Mummy got into a minicab to come and pick me up so that we could go to see her.

As Mummy spoke, fear lodged itself in my tummy. I knew without her saying it that things weren't looking good for Nana Asantewa. As we left, I heard Mrs Pier say, "Don't worry about Esi coming back to school. Just focus on your mother-in-law." It was strange to hear Nana Asantewa being referred to in that way, but I suppose that is who she was.

When Mummy and I arrived at the Oncology ward where Nana was being looked after, Mummy pressed the ward buzzer. The strange hospital smell of disinfectant mixed with something else had me feeling jittery as memories came rushing back of coming to see Mummy in hospital after her accident. A nurse answered the intercom, let us in, and directed us to Nana Asantewa's room.

Mummy knocked on the door. Father opened it, looking drawn, but a smile lit his face when he saw us. "Come in," he said, stepping back.

My eyes were drawn immediately to Nana Asantewa. She was lying with her eyes closed on the hospital bed.

I caught my breath. Was this the same woman I saw only a few days ago? She looked so gaunt as if her flesh had been sucked out, leaving her just skin and bones. Her eyes were sunken and her breathing laboured.

Mummy turned to Father and asked quietly, "Is she asleep?"

"Yes, but you can wake her up. She said to do so before she went to sleep."

Mummy approached the bed and sat on the chair next to it, resting her crutches against the wall. I couldn't bring myself to move any closer.

Mummy said gently, "Mama Asantewa, Esi and I are here."

Nana Asantewa didn't respond.

"Mama Asantewa, can you hear me? It's Maggie. I'm here with Esi."

Still, there was no response, and then slowly Nana Asantewa opened her eyes. She smiled weakly at Mummy.

"Maggie, I am so glad you came. Where is Esi?"

"She's right here," Mummy replied, gesturing for me to move forward. I forced myself to do so.

"Ah, Esi, I am sorry you have to see me like this," Nana Asantewa said, reaching feebly for my hand. "But I'm glad that I am able to say a proper goodbye to you before I run out of time."

I started crying uncontrollably. Mummy put her arm around me and Father moved to stand close. "Don't cry, my dear Esi," Nana Asantewa continued softly. "I thank God that we were able to spend time together. I see so much of me in you and am really proud of you. I'm just sorry we missed out on so much time together and that I won't be around to see you blossom into the amazing woman I know you will be."

I was sobbing loudly by then. Nana Asantewa squeezed my hand slightly as she said, "Remember the good times, Esi, and make the most of your life."

Nana Asantewa closed her eyes for a few moments but kept hold of my hand. I'd managed to rein in my tears when she opened her eyes again.

She gazed at my face and smiled. "Solomon, Maggie, I know that I should keep out of your relationship, but I would die with regret if I didn't tell you what I am about to say."

"What did you want to say, Ma?" Father said gently.

"You and Maggie can't carry on like you are. Neither of you has been able to move on. Yet you're both wasting time."

Mummy looked shocked at Nana Asantewa's words, as did Father. He'd clearly not been expecting Nana Asantewa to say what she said.

"Maggie, please forgive Solomon," Nana continued, looking intently at Mummy. "You can hold onto your hurt and continue to be unhappy, or you can let go of the hurt, forgive, and see what happens with Solomon. I can't make you forgive him but I ask that you be honest with yourself. Because when you are, you'll recognise that what I say is right."

Mummy, looking very emotional, nodded, although it wasn't clear what she was agreeing to.

"Solomon, if Maggie forgives you, you must promise not to betray her again."

Nana Asantewa's blunt words hung in the air. I couldn't read the expression on Father's face.

"So?" Nana Asantewa said, impatiently.

"I promise," said Father gruffly, looking at Mummy's face. "I've been stupid once and paid the price. I wouldn't do it again."

On hearing that, tears started running down Mummy's face, like a tap had been turned on. She rummaged in her handbag and pulled out some tissues.

"I also want you to promise, Solomon," Nana Asantewa added, "that, no matter what, you will start being a proper father to Esi."

Father looked down at me with a serious expression and said, "Esi, from now on, I will be there for you."

Those few words made me weep. Having a *proper* father was something I'd dreamt about for so long. I wept, even more, when Father gathered me in his arms and held me.

Though my tears finally subsided, he kept his arm around me as Nana Asantewa moved on to talk about the letters she'd written for various people. She reminded Father of her instructions about her will and her funeral.

Later that afternoon, at Nana Asantewa's request, the hospital chaplain came to pray with her. Around five pm, Mummy and I bade Nana Asantewa a tearful goodbye and left her and Father at the hospital to go home. Around nine pm, Nana Asantewa died.

When I spoke to Nana Nancy, distraught after Nana Asantewa's death, she sounded sad as she consoled me. She admitted for the first time that she and Nana Asantewa had once been friends, but when Nana Asantewa took sides when Mummy and Father split up, they fell out. She thought that Nana Asantewa had behaved badly until she turned up in London and made amends.

With fresh tears in my eyes, I hear Father announce to those present at the family meeting that, as requested by Nana Asantewa, Father and Grandad Sam would be flying back to Ghana with Nana Asantewa's body. Arrangements were being made but they were hoping to fly out by early December. Her funeral would be held in Kumasi. The dates would be confirmed later.

Wiping away the tears, I turn to Mummy and ask, "Can we go to the funeral? I would really like to be there."

"God willing, Esi," Mummy says, "we'll go. You would be expected to be there as Nana Asantewa's only grandchild. But depending on when it is, we'll have to ask permission from your school before we can go."

I sit back, happy with that.

"When we go, we will, of course, stay with Mama, Ama and Cissy," Mummy adds with a smile.

That makes me grin. Yeah, it'll be wonderful to spend time with Nana, Ama, and Auntie Cissy again. But even as I grin, I'm aware that something has changed in me. The idea of going to Ghana with Mummy and returning with her to London feels okay. I don't have that strong urge anymore to live in Ghana. After Mummy woke up from sedation, I was so grateful that I felt guilty even thinking about living in Ghana. But this feels different. I turn and look at Mummy. *Wow*! I think I'm actually happy living in London with Mummy.

34

It's been over three weeks since Nana Asantewa died.

Mummy is still more affectionate than before the accident and so much easier to talk to.

This Thursday, she went back to work for the first time since her accident. The night before, she was a little anxious, but Father was the one who calmed her down. Father has been spending a lot of time with us. He and Mummy talk a lot now and laugh too, their previous anger amazingly nowhere in sight.

Father took Mummy to her hospital appointment with the consultant on Monday, which is when the cast on her leg was taken off and the consultant gave her the all clear. That evening, as I was about to walk into the living room from the kitchen after dinner, I overheard them talking about Father setting up a standing order to pay Mummy money every month for my upkeep. The amount Father said he would pay was jaw-dropping – it seemed so much, especially as it was in addition to a savings account that Nana had opened in my name before she died. I was touched when he said to Mummy, "I hope this means you won't have to work such long hours."

Mummy smiled at him, a look of appreciation and something else on her face. Then she spotted me at the door and the expression vanished, as she and Father turned their attention to me.

Father has even come to church with us twice since the family meeting. The first time, as soon as Ms Mary saw him, she made a beeline to him, asking about Nana Asantewa's funeral arrangements and profusely expressing her condolences. I could tell that she was dying to know what was going on with Father and Mummy, but Father wouldn't be drawn on the subject.

The second Sunday, after church, Father came to lunch with us at Auntie Comfort's place. Though Nana Asantewa's death was still fresh, it was an enjoyable, relaxed lunch with a lot of laughter.

Last week Friday, when Nana Nancy called in the evening, for the first time, she asked to speak to Father when Mummy told her he was there. Father looked worried when he took the phone, but he spoke to Nana Nancy for quite a while. Afterwards, when Nana spoke to me, she happily said that God was in control and doing his work with Mummy and Father.

Grandad Sam has been more elusive. He only started coming over with Father this week on Tuesday.

When I saw him after school on that day, he didn't appear as distraught as he had been at the family meeting, but he seemed awkward around Mummy and me. On Wednesday, when I arrived home from school, Mummy told me that Grandad had been over without Father and they had had a "good, honest chat," as she put it. The chat must have helped because that evening when he returned with Father, he looked a lot more at ease. He has been insisting on calling me Asantewa, which at first felt strange, but I've started getting used to it and actually quite like it. It makes me feel connected to Nana Asantewa.

Today I've had the most amazing day out with him and Father. To celebrate my fourteenth birthday, which is tomorrow, they took me to Central London as a special treat and showed me a side of London that I've not yet seen.

We went to the South Bank where we had fish and chips in a café by the River Thames. Then, with Father and Grandad Sam on either side of me, we walked along the river gazing at it and taking in the sights, including a graffiti walled skate-park where people were busy skateboarding. A cool breeze blew in our faces as we walked, but I didn't mind. I was too busy enjoying being the focus of Father and Grandad Sam's attention.

This was my first ever outing, that I can remember, with either of them and I was loving it. I listened intently as Grandad Sam spoke about his time in London when he was a student and his subsequent visits when he worked for the Ghana government. He said he hadn't been to London much since he'd retired, but he didn't say anything about why he hadn't accompanied Nana Asantewa to London for her medical treatment. Although I was curious, I didn't feel able to ask in case it upset him.

We went to look at some exhibitions in the Southbank Centre before walking back to the tube station to get the train to a place called Covent Garden. There, we walked for a short while through throngs of people before coming across amazing street performers who we watched for a bit. Father then led us to the Africa Centre, which I'd never even heard of before. At the Centre, I enjoyed looking around the exhibitions of artefacts from different parts of Africa. At the Centre's shop, Father suggested I choose something I liked and he would buy it for me for my birthday. I looked and looked before deciding on a pretty, Kente covered notebook and two books by Ama Ata Aidoo.

Back at the flat, Mummy told me that she had agreed to Father and Grandad Sam coming to a restaurant with us to celebrate my birthday after church tomorrow. From the restaurant, we would be going to Auntie Comfort's flat to have the birthday cake she's baked for me. Mohammed, Karen, and Savaan will be there too. Mummy said that Kojo invited them. That made me really happy. My birthday tomorrow is going to be just amazing with all the people in London who mean the most to me.

Even as I get ready for bed, I can't keep the smile off my face. I turn the light off and snuggle up under the duvet, feeling warm inside.

Mummy and Father wanting to celebrate my birthday together (along with Grandad Sam, who I'm getting to know), is by far my best birthday present ever. Having a mother and father who get along has been something that for a long time I thought I'd never have. When I left Ghana, I never imagined that this would be happening. I wonder if Nana Asantewa knew that her words from her deathbed would result in this? I'm sure if she's looking down now, she is happy.

Father and Grandad Sam are going back to Ghana soon with Nana Asantewa's body, but I'm hopeful that things won't return to the way they were. I have the trip to Ghana with Mummy to look forward to. Nana Asantewa's funeral will be difficult. Even thinking about it makes me sad. But on the positive side, I'm sure I'll get to spend time with Father and Grandad Sam. Of course, I can't wait to see Nana Nancy, Auntie Cissy, and Ama. It will be wonderful to be back in Nana's house, my old bedroom and the bakery. I plan to eat as much of Nana's cake and bread as is humanly possible. Yes, I'm going to enjoy my visit to Ghana.

Thinking of Ghana reminds me of how anxious I felt about moving to London. My time here has *definitely* had its challenges, but the fact that I've managed to cope with everything that has happened makes me realise that I'm actually a *pretty* strong person. "Thank you, God," I whisper clasping my hands together, "for giving me the strength to get through the last few months ... and for helping Mummy and Father to get on better."

I've gained much more than I ever expected when I left Ghana. So now, even though I don't know what the future holds, I'm not worried because somehow, I know with God's help, I'll be okay.

Yes, life is looking up!

NOTES

1. Akan – is the principal language of the Akan people of Ghana and is spoken by the majority of Ghanaians. Akan is made up of several dialects including Twi and Fanti. The Akan language spoken in this book is Twi.

2. *Da n'ase, Da n'ase, Da Onyame ase* means, in Twi, thank him, thank him, thank God.

3. *Kaba* and *Sleet* are traditional Ghanaian attire worn by women consisting of a top (Kaba) and matching long skirt (Sleet).

4. Accra is the capital city of Ghana.

5. *Wo kɔ tena aburokyire* means, in Twi, you are going to live abroad.

6. *Kotoka airport is an international airport in Accra.*

7. Kenkey is a boiled, fermented corn dough ball eaten in Ghana.

8. Shito is a hot pepper sauce eaten in Ghana.

9. *Akwaaba* means, in Twi, welcome.

10. Tema is a port city in Ghana near Accra.

11. Achimota, East Legon and Tesano are suburbs of Accra.

12. Yam is a starchy, edible tuber grown and eaten in Ghana.

13. Kontomire is a stew made with cocoyam leaves eaten in Ghana. Ghanaians abroad sometimes use spinach if they cannot get hold of cocoyam leaves.

14. *Bubu* is a long, loose-fitting, brightly coloured garment popular in West Africa.

15. Use of Aunty and Uncle – In Ghanaian society, saying Aunty or Uncle is a respectful way of addressing an adult who is older than you, even if you are not related to them.

16. *Waakye* is a Ghanaian dish of rice and beans.

17. *Nyame, hwe Esi ma me* means, in Twi, God, look after Esi for me

18. *Highlife is* Ghanaian dance music which retains the melodies and rhythmic structures of traditional Akan music but has evolved with the trends and technology of pop culture.

19. Hiplife music is a Ghanaian musical style which fuses highlife music and some elements of hip-hop.

20. *Maadu* means, in Twi, I have arrived.

21. *Buns* bread is a sweet Ghanaian bread.

22. *Kafra* means, in Twi, sorry.

23. *Gyae su* means, in Twi, stop crying.

24. *Wahala* is West African slang for trouble or worries.

25. *Brebiara ye* means, in Twi, everything is okay.

26. *Mepa wo kyɛw* means, in Twi, please.

27. Labadi Beach in Accra is a popular beach next to the Atlantic Ocean.

28. *Medaase* means, in Twi, thank you.

29. Milo is a brand of hot chocolate popular in Ghana.

30. Chale is Ghanaian slang for "my friend or man."

31. *Wo mbu ade* means, in Twi, you are disrespectful.

32. *Don't bring yourself* is Ghanaian slang for stop grandstanding, being smug or self-important.

33. *Nti na woyɛɛ anopa yi ɛkyerɛ sɛn* means, in Twi, what was the point of what you did this morning.

34. *Tɔ wo bo ase* means, in Twi, exercise patience.

35. Mogadishu is the capital city of Somalia.

36. *Inshallah* means if Allah wills it (Arabic Islamic).

37. Korle-bu hospital is a teaching hospital in Ghana's capital city, Accra.

38. Cedi is the currency used in Ghana.

39. Kumasi is a city in the Ashanti region of Ghana. It is Ghana's second city after Accra.

40. Kente cloth is woven from silk and comes in many different colours. It is Ghana's national cloth.

About the Author

Educated up to PhD, Abena Eyeson lives in a leafy suburb just outside London with her husband and three young children. Between school runs, managing a busy household and trying to maintain a working life, her love for drama and writing led her to pen *Looking Up*, her debut novel.

"I'm always eager for my readers to communicate with me. I would appreciate your feedback and would love for you to write a review. If this book was bought through Amazon or another online bookshop, please post your review on their website. Otherwise, use my website www.abenaeyesonwrites.com to send me your feedback and to subscribe for updates.

Thanks for reading Looking Up xx."

Printed in Great Britain
by Amazon